Marji's Books

The Christmas Tree Treasure Hunt

Grime Fighter Series
Grime Beat

Grime Wave

Grime Spree

Grime Family

Grime & Punishment

Heath's Point Suspense
Counter Point

Breaking Point

Boiling Point (coming soon)

Flash Point (coming soon)

Dallas Duets Clean Billionaire Romance
Ain't Misbehaving

Cry Me a River (coming soon)

Puttin' on the Ritz (coming soon)

Grime Spree

**Grime Fighter Mystery
Book #3**

Marji Laine

Grime Spree
Second Edition
© 2019 Marji Laine
ISBN: 978-1-944120-93-1

This book is a work of fiction. Names, characters, places, and incidents are either products of the author's imagination or used fictitiously. Any similarity to actual people and/or events is purely coincidental.

Scriptures marked "ESV" are from The Holy Bible, English Standard Version ® (ESV ®), copyright © 2001 by Crossway, a publishing ministry of Good News Publishers. Used by permission. All rights reserved.

Scriptures marked "KJV" are from The Holy Bible, the Authorized (King James) Version.

Faith Driven Book Production Services
Find out more about the author: *Marji Laine.com*
Or email her at: *AuthorMarjiLaine@gmail.com*

Printed in the United States of America.

I appreciate the way my
sweet family works together
to make life easy for me,
especially when I'm on the
edge of a new release!

I dedicate this book to my daughter,
the oldest of my twins by eleven minutes.

Breana
Beautiful, Talented
Laughing, Creating, Serving
Follows the Lord's Leading
Devoted

The Lord has poured out such blessing
with this amazing lady,
and she still calls me Mommy!

*Have nothing to do with
the fruitless deeds of darkness,
but rather expose them.
It is shameful even to mention what the
disobedient do in secret.
Ephesians 5:11-12*

Chapter One

Dani Foster observed herself in the mirror on the back of her closet door. Surely the mirror had to be lying. The dress she'd ordered from that New York boutique could not look like a tent with a drawstring.

She lifted a wide black belt from the organized hanger in the corner of her closet and wrapped it around her waist, bringing the hem to just above her knees. That looked better. She pivoted. Good even.

"Violet is a perfect color for you." Her roommate, Tasha, assessed her from the open bedroom doorway. "Jay's eyes are going to pop."

"I don't know about that." She pursed her lips together, suppressing a bubble of anticipation, and smoothed a long brown wave behind her ear.

"Don't pretend with me." Tasha wandered to the open closet. "I know you're crazy over that man. And he's nuts about you, too." She fingered through the mostly informal shirts and jeans that made up Dani's wardrobe. She pulled out a royal blue silk blouse that matched her eyes.

Dani refocused on her reflection and dabbed at her eyelids with a liner. Enough makeup to make the most of her assets without painting herself. Her eyes weren't the striking blue of Tasha's or the chocolate of Jay's, though their dark color did make them look large and expressive. Her hair was almost the same color. She'd fought it for a while but was glad she'd gone back to her natural color after years of being a platinum blonde. "Jay and I are simply getting to know each other. No promises or commitments."

"Not yet." Tasha moved toward the mirror and

held the blouse under her chin, her yellow ringlets tumbling against the blue for an enchanting effect. "Wish I had a guy getting to know me."

Shifting her focus, Dani stared at her friend's reflection. With her perfect figure and constant energy, the girl should have dozens of guys after her. "You wait. You'll have tons of lawyer types chasing you in no time."

That urged out a giggle. "Maybe." She hung the garment on the doorknob. "I have to graduate first. Then there's the bar exam. Et cetera. Et Cetera."

Dani snatched up the blouse. "I predict four different guys in your life by this time next year." She found the blueish section of her closet and shoved some hangers aside to insert the one she held. After flattening the sides of the fabric, she evenly spacing the hangers again.

"I barely know four men—your guy, Carla's guy, the pastor, and our boss—and I know you aren't talking about any of them."

"I'm not talking family, Tash. And especially not Frank. Eww." Their boss at Kellerman Crisis and Trauma Cleaning was egotistical, self-absorbed, and had the compassion of a mosquito. "Next year, you'll have your degree, maybe even an office at some exceptional law firm."

"Ooh. If only." Tasha pulled the sides of her bouncy hair back and angled to the side. "I'll need a more professional style."

"You should wear it flat-ironed like you did at church last week. Gorgeous." Dani shifted her fake ID and credit cards to a smaller purse and hung the other one in the back of the closet. After smoothing her comforter and straightening the pillow, she followed her friend into the living room.

"Took a while, but it was worth it." Tasha paused at the tablet on the TV stand where a scanner application transmitted a call from the Dallas Police dispatch. "Uh, oh. Hope your fella doesn't bail on you again."

Dani halted. Surely not. He'd promised this

time.

Tasha turned up the volume on a female voice. "Two-four-five, remain. Back-up ETA three minutes."

"They found a body near White Rock Lake." She tilted her head. "At least I think that's what they said."

Great. Right around the corner from Jay's department. Dani slumped. "So much for this date."

"You can't expect the worst."

Easy for her to say. He'd canceled several already. "What can I expect when I'm dating a cop? Or not dating, as the case may be." She'd hardly seen him in more than two weeks.

"Wait, let me listen. Maybe one of the other teams will process the scene." Tasha turned the sound a little louder.

"He only recently got his promotion. Of course he's going to opt to lead any crime scene investigation that he can." Served her right. She had no business getting involved with anyone.

Especially not a policeman. "Might as well change out of these clothes." Stomping into her room, she resisted the urge to slam her bedroom door but did throw her purse on the comforter.

She flounced onto the blanket folded at the foot of her bed. On one of their rare, successful dates, Jay had found the Native American weave in blues and grays at a trading market. She fingered the broad chevrons. If only she'd not already lost her heart to that man. She'd forgive him, of course. He'd make it up to her with another date, though the jury would be out if he'd keep that one. Big cities could be violent from time to time. Especially during the summer.

She felt, rather than heard, the front door open. The sudden draft sucked her door to its facing.

"I'll get her." Tasha's voice.

Dani flew to her mirror to check her mascara. Tears had threatened but not fallen. Thank goodness.

Tasha tapped on the door as Dani collected the

small bag from the bed and spread out the wrinkle she'd made where she'd been sitting. Her friend poked her nose in. "Guess he didn't take that crime scene after all." She grinned and winked at her.

Dani pumped her fists at the ceiling before composing herself and joining her fellow in the living room. Her heart danced as it often did when she caught sight of his smile.

"You look beautiful. As always." His tan, deepened from the summer sun, highlighted his ultra-white smile. He slipped his arm around her waist and kissed her temple as she neared.

"You're not so bad yourself." Not bad. Ha. He was drop-dead gorgeous. His short, black hair and tanned complexion gave him the warrior appearance of his Comanche ancestors. But the lighter brown of his eyes, with a sparkle that made her insides tingle, betrayed his mother's European background. Wasn't she Scottish? Dani couldn't remember.

With his arm draped around her shoulders,

they made their way out the door.

Tasha gave her a thumbs-up as she reached the staircase. Surely, this date would be a good one. It was certainly starting out that way.

Jay Hunter watched as Dani preceded him down the stairs, her dark hair swinging slightly and bouncing with every step. Passing off that last minute call had been the right move.

How had he garnered the attention of such a beauty? And smart. And fun.

She paused at the bottom of the steps and turned to look up at him, her left hand clasping her right elbow behind her back. A sure sign of her nerves. But what did she have to be nervous about. Surely, she knew how he felt about her.

He hurried down the stairs. "Are you hungry?"

"Famished. Crackers and peanut butter for lunch." She climbed into the passenger seat of his gun-metal gray Dodge Charger and glanced up at him. "Hope you have plenty of credit."

Her eyes sparkled with her little joke. The look she gave made his chest lurch. The way her lips pressed together making a little dimple appear when she was about to say something clever. He jogged around the back of the car and got in on his side, cranking the engine as he settled into his seat.

Immediately, his radio transmitted another call. "Coroner's office is in route. Confirm arrival."

He'd been monitoring the discussion from the response team that had taken the scene of a newly found body. "Sorry about that." He turned down the sound.

"Tasha and I heard it over the scanner app on my tablet." She glanced out the side window. "Thought you might have taken the call."

His collar tightened around his neck. A trickle of sweat drifted the width of his forehead before he wiped at it with the back of his hand. Truth was, had it not been for his partner, he probably would have gone. He needed as much experience leading the investigation teams as he could get. "Cal's team is out on it, but Sergeant Lasaures took lead on it."

"You sound disappointed." She twisted toward him.

He glanced at her for a second then averted his gaze through the windshield. "I'm disappointed that another case had to happen during one of our dates. I'm disappointed that I'm going to miss out on working it. But I'm not sad that made the decision to come get you. To keep this date. I've been looking forward to having you to myself for a few hours."

She laid soft fingertips on top of his hand where it rested on his gear shift. "I've been looking forward to this as well. When the call came over."

"You expected the worst?"

"You working a case isn't the worst." She stroked his hand with her thumb. "But I wasn't thrilled with the prospect of having to reschedule yet again."

"I know it's been hard for you. It won't always be like this. I'm busy because I'm just starting out. That's all."

She shook her head. "No. This isn't hard for me. I'm not complaining. Really. I'm glad for you and what you've accomplished." She shrugged. "I miss you sometimes, though."

He pulled to an intersection and stopped at the red light. With her chin down, she looked as much a shy teenager as she did a confident twenty-eight-year-old woman who had taken on a murderer and a kidnapper in the last several months.

Turning his hand, he laced his fingers with hers. "I miss visiting with you after work. New position, new schedule. Hopefully, as I get tenured, I adjust my times and drop by like I used to."

The light changed, forcing him to release her hand.

The schedule wasn't the real problem. She knew it. She had to. His new position whet his appetite again to impress his dad, a long-time sheriff in their East Texas County. But which did he want more? The job or the girl? And could he really have both? His father had.

"I thought we'd do Italian tonight. If you're up for it."

Her head turned toward the window again. "Sounds lovely."

Her lack of enthusiasm disheartened him. Was he crazy to think he could have both an amazing relationship with the woman of his dreams and a job that fulfilled him? "Would you rather do Mexican? We could go downtown."

"No. I like Italian." Still she stared out her window.

He took a main artery toward the upscale strip center in a prestigious northern section of the city. Good thing she had a taste for Italian. Cancelling the reservations after ignoring that call and everything would have been a pain. He parked near the end of a strip of multi-retail buildings. With a stonework facade and wrought iron fixtures, the place declared the excessive nature of the developer.

"La Bella Nodo?" She turned wide eyes toward him. "I've heard so much about this place."

"Me, too. Thought it was time to try it." He tilted his head toward her. "I told you I owed you big after I had to break the last date."

"Yes, but I didn't expect you to go bankrupt over it."

He helped her out of the car and tucked her hand into the corner of his arm. They had the length of the building to walk to get to the entrance. He should have opted for valet parking. Next time he'd think of that sooner. Reaching the entrance, he released her long enough to hold the glass-panel door open. They stepped into candle-lit opulence.

Piano music drifted through the large dining room. The tables, tucked into discrete sections, lined the windows at the front of the building and settled in between the patio doors along the narrow wall. On the piazza, outside the open doorways, several couples danced on a paneled floor surrounded by twinkle lights and what looked like a small garden.

No wonder the two female cops he'd worked with last week had gone on about this place. A glance at Dani's face told him their advice had been exactly right.

Chapter Two

La Bella Nodo reminded Dani of romantic movies. Not that she enjoyed the icky-sweet stories so much, but Tasha did. The two of them had watched several over the last weekend when her previous date had fallen through.

This place more than repaid her temporary disappointment.

"Is this your first time?" A host leveled a partial smile in her direction.

She ignored the man's pointed look. Had he meant to say it so suggestively? She stared at his black sneakers. "This is quite a place."

Jay stepped behind her, his hand to her back. "I have a reservation for two under the name of Hunter."

She glanced again at the host. His cleanly shaved head reflected some of the dim lights around him, but his piercing dark eyes hadn't left her face.

"I see, Mr. Hunter. If you'll follow me." Only then did his concentrated stare break.

What was that about? An alarm, from her many months in witness protection, went off inside her head. Yet, he couldn't know who she was. She looked nothing like the pampered, spoiled girl she'd left behind in California. And why would anyone look for her here of all places?

He looked back at her and winked.

Eww. She paused and grabbed her right elbow behind her back.

If Jay had noticed, he didn't show any reaction. Maybe he didn't care that some creep was flirting with his date? Nah. Any guy would care about that, if nothing than for the pride of the matter. She released her hold on her arm and wrapped her fingers around his.

He glanced her direction and covered her hand with his own. "What do you think?"

"Amazing." Atmosphere—five stars. Personnel—negative three. The food would have to make up for the guy leading their journey through the room.

He stopped at a table near the bar. "Here we are." He held out a chair. "For the *bella signorina*."

"What does that mean?" Dani moved to the chair, wishing Jay had been holding it.

"Beautiful lady." Jay took the seat across from her. "And I agree."

The host nudged her chair forward. "*Sei bellisima*." His whisper warmed her shoulder into a skin crawl. Then he hurried away.

She wiped her neck. Ick. "What does bellisima mean?"

Jay pulled at the knot in his napkin, but halted and stared at her. "Did that guy say that to you?"

"Yes. Whispered it. Very creepy." She shuddered.

He raised his left eyebrow and looked in the direction the man had gone. "It means he thinks you're hot."

Eww again. Her mouth dropped open for a moment. "Well, that's degrading."

Once again, he glanced toward the front of the dining room. "Probably his attempt at charm." Then his gaze rested on her, and a tender look of appreciation settled across his features. He reached across the table to cover her hand with his. "I guess he couldn't help himself. And I can't say I blame him."

Swoon. How did she respond to that?

Tiny wrinkles showed in the corners of his eyes. "Though I would have used something like *bella tesora.*" His voice grew husky with the accent.

Her stomach whirled somewhere around her shoulders. She took a deep breath. "What's the difference?"

He gave a slight shrug and stroked the back of her hand with his thumb. "What he said focused only on your physical attractiveness, but I know your inner light as well. Bella tesora—beautiful treasure."

Yeah? "I don't know what to say." This man was beyond amazing.

His gaze dropped to the table for a moment. "Say you'll come with me to Marseille?"

Huh? "Who's Marcie?" Was she a sister or something?

"*What* is the better question." He gave her hand a squeeze, released it, and slid his napkin into his lap. "Marseille, like the place in France, only in East Texas, we don't pronounce it right, so it sounds more like Marcie. It's where I grew up. My parents throw a big Fourth of July celebration every year."

Oh wait. His parents? No, no, no. Meeting parents wasn't part of her path. Not with...

everything she still had to do. Besides, she couldn't up and leave Dallas like that. Or could she?

The butterflies that had been winging their way inside her turned to wasps.

"My whole family will be there. My brothers and their wives and kids. And you'll love my sister. She'll have a little one early next year."

"In Marseille?"

"Beautiful place." His eyes warmed. "Near Caddo Lake in the heart of the piney woods. Green and fresh. My dad's retired from the sheriff's department. Has some cattle and a stock pond. And my mom will love showing you her garden. Seriously, gardening is a sport to her."

"On July Fourth." Try as she might, she couldn't think of any excuses to bow out of the trip. Not something she was at liberty to actually explain.

"I've already taken the weekend off. Since they owe me, like, weeks of vacation time, the captain didn't think it would pose much of a problem."

Wait. Her job. "I'm not sure I can do that."

"Tyrone said y'all always get off on the big three holidays—the Fourth, Christmas, and Thanksgiving."

That was right. They'd even gotten lucky and had New Year's off. "It's… I mean…."

"You're nervous about meeting my family." He scanned her face. "Guess it isn't all that fair since you don't have any local family for me to meet."

She released a sigh. "I'm not sure I'm ready."

"I think…." He gazed into her eyes again. "Make that, I *know* I care about you. And I believe you feel the same. My family is an important part of my life. I want to give them a chance to fall in… to get to know you like I have."

His gentle voice and tender look incapacitated her resolve. "I really would like to go. If we can work out the details." She had gotten far too good at lying. Should she and Jay have a chance at any future, she'd have to break that trend.

Of course, Matthew would never allow such. At least, he'd give her a reasonable excuse she could use to get out of it.

A waiter hovered behind Jay. Dani looked up and had a sharp intake of breath. That man. She knew him. And his stare—first curious, then with widened eyes—confirmed he recognized her as well.

Dani stared into Tonio's dark gaze.

He arched a thick eyebrow in her direction and tilted his head toward the hallway on her left labeled with the word *Salon* in a swirling font.

"I've heard everything here is outstanding." Jay turned the thick page of the menu.

Behind him, Tonio's eyes pierced her. Again, he bobbed his head toward her left. His spiked black hair quivered with the movement.

She hazarded a glance around the dining room. Were any of the *others* here? When her gaze met back with Tonio's, he'd completed pouring water at the neighboring table. His eyes were slits, and his bottom lip had rolled between his teeth.

Dani startled. It had been a year since she'd seen his particular type of silent insistence. And witnessed the repercussions of failure to obey. "I'll be right back." She could only hope. She laid her napkin across the chair cushion and picked up her purse.

The hallway lay in front of her. Though she'd lost track of Tonio, doubtless, he hadn't lost track of her. And he wouldn't hesitate to hurt Jay to force her into his will. None of the men she'd known would think twice about an ancillary casualty. Especially if that casualty were a cop.

She proceeded around a corner. A hand shot from the shadows behind a plastic ficus and clamped over her mouth, while a muscular arm wrapped around her waist. She focused on the arm, sinking her stubby nails into it and pushing against her captor, but the man only tightened his hold.

"I'm trying to help you, stupid." Tonio's whisper sounded more hiss-like than she remembered. "Settle down, Sammi. You gotta get outta here." The Brooklyn accent and the sound of her real name jolted her. She stilled, and he loosened his hold.

"What's going on?" She drew her fingers around her lips to remove the feel of his rough hand.

"Nothing you need to know about, but if you don't get out of here, and fast, someone else might see you. Someone who's not as kind as I am."

Ice crawled down her back. "Can't you do anything? Stop whatever it is from happening?" She peeked toward the front, keeping the wall between her Jay.

"Yeah." He took her arm and propelled her farther down the hallway. "I can get you away from this place."

He pushed open the flapping door into the

kitchen and scanned the area. Apparently, this was a little-used entry. All of the cooks and waiters were busy on the far side of the room.

"What about Jay?"

"That guy you're with?" He shoved her past a couple of freezer-lock doors. "I'll try, but no promises."

"I'm not going anywhere without him." She stiffened. No way she was going to leave him to deal with these guys. And with his sense of chivalry, he'd get himself killed trying to play super-cop. "I'm serious."

He opened the door to a broad delivery alley between two legs of the shopping center. "Okay, okay. You stay out here and pretend to barf." He darted back into the building.

She didn't have to pretend. Seeing Tonio ruined her stomach. Her only salvation was that she hadn't eaten yet.

Thankfully, he had been the one to happen upon her. He'd been the only member of the network to be nice. She didn't have a prayer if any of the others saw her.

God, please don't let that happen. She had finally begun to feel at home here. Moving again would break her heart.

And please take care of Jay.

Chapter Three

Jay had caught a glimpse of Dani's face as she exited the dining room. She'd looked over the room, or so it seemed, before ducking into that hallway.

He followed the trail of her gaze. Waiters in service tuxedos moved with grace and calm through the room. Some carried large round trays high over their heads. Others, with a signature towel over their forearms, poured from carafes or opened bottles of wine. Patrons, mostly in pairs at widely separated tables, had intimate conversations in the candlelight.

Like he should be having with Dani.

And he would be, had she not scurried out. That woman was nothing if not mysterious. Hopefully, this visit to his parents' ranch would prove his intentions and convince her to trust him with her past.

It couldn't be that bad. She was such a kind-hearted woman, raised by a detective father—a cop if he'd made the correct conclusions from the rare details that had slipped into some of their conversations.

And she loved the Lord. He'd seen that for himself each time they had discussed truth from the Bible and the one time she'd visited his church with him.

Though being a Christian didn't make her immune to trouble.

The fact was, a woman who avoided open, honest conversations would never have gained his attention in the past. And Dani's evasion troubled him constantly, yet something compelled him to stay with her. Who would think that he, of all people, would be falling for a woman who wasn't completely above-board in all areas?

He needed to find a way to speak to the Lord about her, but he was convinced God wanted him to give her up. Her with her secret past and baggage.

That conversation was for another time, though.

The menu blurred in front of his eyes. The woman was amazing, but that didn't mean she'd always been that way. Maybe a change in her character had been brought about by something heinous.

He'd be wise not to contemplate the possibilities of her secrets. Doubtless, his imagination would conjure something much worse that what actually shamed her.

He shut the menu. His eyes fell on the elaborate font on the elegant cover. La Bella Noda. The beautiful knot? Strange name for a restaurant. He looked to his right at the hallway Dani had taken. She'd been gone a while.

A waiter hurried toward him, glanced to his right and slowed his stride to an almost casual gait. He pulled out his pad as he neared. "You're Jay?" The low rumble of the room swallowed the man's husky voice, so that no one else could have heard it.

The cop inside Jay alerted, and he met the man's dark eyes. He gave a tentative nod.

"Your friend, Sammi, is sick."

"You mean Dani?" He stood, squinting into the hallway where Dani had disappeared.

"Dani, yeah. And she didn't wanna come back into the dining room, ya know." He pointed toward the bathroom wing.

"Where is she?"

The man, obviously Italian, started down the hallway. Jay followed his bulk—about an inch taller and at least 100 pounds of muscle heavier than Jay—down the same corridor where Dani had disappeared. The guy took him through a section of the kitchen and peeked out a back door before opening it wide.

The rock facing of the building continued about twenty yards dead-ending into a high wooden fence with a gate latch on one panel. Dani, bent double, leaned away from him near the gate.

"Honey, what happened?" He stepped toward her, but the waiter grabbed his arm.

"You need your car." He pulled Jay away and directed him down the alley toward the parking lot.

Jay snatched his phone from his pocket. "I'm thinking along the lines of an ambulance."

"No!" Both Dani and the waiter answered in tandem.

"Take me home. Please." Dani didn't look at him, but her weak voice tripped-up his resolve.

"I'll be right back." Jay bolted from them down the long alley.

He'd never played football in high school, but he'd usually medaled in track. Sprint had been his specialty, though he puffed by the time he reached his car. Too many hours at the computer.

Hopefully he wouldn't regret not calling an ambulance right away, but he could still take Dani to the hospital if needed.

Only a few minutes had passed, but the waiter had disappeared by the time Jay returned. How could he have just left her like that?

As he neared, she straightened and moved away from the wall. Without giving Jay the chance to help her in, Dani grabbed the door handle, jerking the door open. Then she leaped into the passenger seat. "Go." She doubled over again.

Her acrobatics hadn't been those of someone sick, but he didn't want to argue with her. Instead, he made her sit up far enough for him to latch her seatbelt around her. Then, he stepped on the gas and took a left out of the alley and into the lot. "When did you start feeling bad?"

She raised her head slightly and peered out the passenger window. "Um… I was fine until we got to the restaurant." She buried her face against her knees but not before he noticed the pallor of her skin.

"I'm taking you to the closest emergency room."

"You can't." She lifted her head for an instant, then cast a glance out the window before ducking again.

That's what she was doing... ducking. "A clinic then. If you're sick. You need a doctor."

"No. I just need to go home."

Jay paused at the exit to the center. "Violently throwing up after you're perfectly healthy?" Had she actually been throwing up? "Either you need a doctor, or we need to have a talk."

"Please, can you just drive?"

The alarms on the edges of his brain blared. Dani's secrets mushroomed like an atom bomb, but his discussion with her could wait. At least until she calmed down a little.

He turned onto the main thoroughfare and

drove a quarter mile. "Are you feeling any better?" Maybe he could ease her into explaining her actions?

She lifted her head for a moment before letting her shoulders lower as she relaxed. "I'll be okay."

Whatever she was hiding from—and she'd been plainly hiding—seemed to have passed. But the charade had to end. He directed the Charger to an empty parking lot in front of what had once been a grocery store and moved the gear into park.

"What are you doing?" She lifted her head and scanned the area. "I want to go home."

"Why? What has you so scared?"

She stared at him. "You saw me. I'm sick."

"I saw you play sick. What is really going on? Who are you hiding from?" So much for the gentle urging he'd intended. After all, she'd been keeping things from him since they'd met.

She straightened in her seat and cast another nervous glance through the windshield. "Take me home, Jay. There are some things you simply wouldn't understand."

"Try me. I'm a pretty understanding guy."

Her features softened for a moment as she turned her gaze to him. "Yes, you are." Then, she dropped her focus to the floorboard. "But I can't explain."

His radio, silent since he'd gotten in the car, sprang into life. "All units in the vicinity of 14451 North Highway, please respond. Reported 211 in progress, code 2."

As the dispatcher continued, he gave Dani a hard stare. Did she have anything to do with the robbery going on in the center they had just left? He pointed to the radio. "Is that what you're hiding from?"

She straightened. "You don't understand." Her reddened face told him enough.

He growled out an exhale. "I understand that I'm needed elsewhere." He moved to shift the gear.

"Wait. No. I can't go back there." She unlatched her seatbelt.

The car had begun to move slowly forward, but he stomped on the brake causing it to jerk. "I'm not going to leave you here." No way. "What sort of man do you think I am?"

Still, he couldn't let her delay him any longer, either.

She pointed across the street. "Bus Stop." She opened her door. "I'll be fine." Shutting it behind her, she jogged to the curb without looking back.

"Fine." He resisted the urge to stomp on the gas as he pulled into the street going the opposite direction. Instead, he reported his location and turned on the strobing lights in his Charger's grill.

Yet he couldn't keep his imagination in check. What had Dani gotten into?

After crossing the street, Dani frowned at the illumination from Jay's lighted, unmarked car. He had no choice about returning to the scene. She didn't blame him. But then, neither did she have a choice. Her return could compromise both of them and get them both killed.

Taking a seat on the covered bench of the bus stop, she scanned the neighborhood. Lots of cars. A couple of pedestrians on the other street walked toward the setting sun. No one glanced in her direction.

And why should they? She wasn't Sammi Fellows. Not anymore. Hadn't been for a year. She'd gone back to her natural hair color instead of the white-blonde she'd had since middle school. She'd even used extensions until it grew out.

She rubbed her forehead with her dry fingertips. No amount of lotion helped what the harsh cleaning chemicals did to her hands. She didn't even buff her fingernails anymore, let alone paint them. And the pencil-thin eyebrows she'd always meticulously maintained were now quite thick.

In fact, the only things about Sammi Fellows

that remained were her memories. Her dad wouldn't have recognized her, by looks or by her actions. Wait, he probably would. Tonio had. How, she couldn't fathom.

Still, she had a feeling her dad would be more proud of the woman she'd become, even as a crime scene cleaner, than the primped, spoiled socialite she was beginning to be before....

She couldn't let her emotions have reign. Not now. Now, when the end of this nightmare was so close. Surely, it would be the end.

The yellow DART bus jostled along the street toward her. She stood as it neared. She'd have to come up with some explanation for Jay. Her WIT-SEC agent kept telling her that no relationship would last through this. But she wanted to prove him wrong.

Especially to keep a guy as amazing as Jay.

The bus slowed as it neared the stop. Suddenly, a hand wrapped around her waist. "There you are, baby."

Tonio gave her a hard glare. His tone dropped to a whisper. "No sudden moves." His right hand, shoved into the pocket of a gray warm-up jacket, waved slightly, and the corner had a sharp edge from something inside the pocket. Something that Tonio brought closer to her waist.

The doors of the bus opened. Dani climbed the steps. "Does this bus go to Almidoor Street?" She'd made up the name hoping no such place existed. Anything to get the man's attention enough to look at her panicked face.

The driver pointed to the sign above him directing travelers not to speak to him. Tonio shoved her up the steps and slid a pass through the notch before urging her to the back of the bus.

They passed a mom and her three daughters chattering about the Perot Museum. Could she get the lady's attention? But if she did, wouldn't that put her and her kids into danger?

She moved on. "Why are you doing this?" She made sure those at the front couldn't hear her.

He moved her to the far seat and settled next to her, tucking his green duffel under his feet before answering. "Needed an alternate exit. But I didn't expect to find you at the stop."

"Okay. I didn't see anything, and I don't know anything." Dani crossed her arms against the gymnastics going on in her stomach as she recited the phrases that were just as untrue now as they had been before she'd moved to Dallas.

"That's real good. I can work with that." He propped his left ankle across his knee. "So where do we get off?"

"Oh, no. I'm not going anywhere with you."

"I'm simply seeing you home, sweetheart. Wouldn't do for me to leave you like this. Not in this neighborhood."

Arguing would get her nowhere. She clammed up and watched for her stop.

Chapter Four

Jay shut off his lights as he neared the restaurant. He parked well away from the building, hemming in two other cars, and walked quickly toward a phone store opposite the doors to La Bella Noda.

Out of view from the diners or anyone else, he jogged to the wall, neared the first window, and pulled out his Sig Sauer. He squatted beneath the glass and lifted his phone camera for a view of the interior.

Not a soul in sight from this angle, though filled plates were cooling on a waiter's tray. Three tables were in view, each with unfinished meals.

A uniformed officer darted toward him.

"Hunter. Sergeant from Northeast Department." Jay kept his eyes on the window, but nothing moved in the interior.

The Hispanic man who had joined him responded in kind as he unholstered his weapon. "Gutierrez, from the South Central division." He made a short report into his radio as Jay moved to the next window. Again, no people. A spilled glass of wine and a chair on its back compelled him to hurry. He skipped looking through the next two windows and moved to the one outside the entrance.

The glass doors were behind a brick corner, hidden from view, but the clear glass gave a vantage point to most of the entry hall. It, too, appeared abandoned. Not even the bald host stood at the podium.

By then, two other officers had joined his train. He pointed to Gutierrez, then to himself and whispered, "We're to the back." Pointing to the other pair, he added, "Wait for my call to enter."

All nodded. Jay turned toward the front of the building and raised three fingers. Lowering one at a time, he pulled his last one into a fist and took off, keeping low as he darted around the rock facade and into full view of the restaurant entrance. He ducked behind a low wall on the opposite side of the patio and made room for Gutierrez.

Jay peered over the wall, and inspected the interior of the entrance. The sunset shown in the reflection of the glass, and its rays illuminated much of the room. No one there, either. Where were all of the people that had filled the place not so long ago?

The worst answer hovered in the back of his mind. *God, please don't let them all be dead.*

Staying behind the wall, he crossed the length of the patio. Where the wall ran into the wooden fence, he hurdled the stone barrier and followed the vine-covered wooden planks to the gate he'd seen from the other side when Dani was sick. Supposedly sick.

He wiped her from his mind.

The hinges squeaked as he shifted the latch and pulled the door open. The alley was as it had been some twenty minutes before. The back door they had used hung slightly open. Didn't it have a hydraulic closer or had it been like that when the waiter led him through it? He leaned against the wall and scanned what he could see of the door. Sure enough, someone had busted the bar away from the piston.

Again with the camera on his phone, he took in the lighted kitchen. Lots of places to hide in there, but waiting outside wouldn't solve that issue. He signaled to Gutierrez to make the call to the others, counted off to three, jerked open the door, and pointed his weapon. The older officer followed, covering Jay's nine-o'clock.

The likelihood of any of the robbers still being inside was slim, but caution and training ruled. He slid behind the grills and pivoted around the island workstation, aiming at the ground, where someone might have been hiding. Might have been, but wasn't.

Someone pushed through the flapping door at Jay's right, the main entrance to the kitchen. He halted and aimed, looking down the muzzle of another handgun held by a woman in blue. She pulled her gun into ready position as did he before he indicated the other entrance. She fell into step behind him.

Gutierrez had already shifted in that direction, retracing the way that Jay had taken to get to Dani earlier. The older officer bypassed the meat-locker type doors and edged open the one leading into that back hallway. He was met by another man in blue who whispered, "Clear."

Jay paused at the first of the three doors. The robbers were long gone. Of that he was sure, yet he lifted his gun and tugged on the first door.

His heart dropped to his heels as a dozen or

more bodies came into view.

"So what is this all about, Tonio?" Dani eyed the man's unnaturally pointed jacket pocket. Gun or knife?

"Let's simply say that I missed my ride, shall we? Since the blame lies basically on you, is it not reasonable that you should make it right?"

"My fault. You're crazy."

"Ah... no. Delayed, I was, after finally coaxing your boyfriend to go get his car. That man is thick-headed. Is he not?" Tonio turned a crooked smile on her. "But he's obviously your ex- now, isn't he?"

Maybe if she kept him talking she could learn what he wanted. "Why would you say that?"

"The scoundrel abandoned you." He straightened and used the theatrical accent he'd always practiced. "Cad." Slumping again, he lifted a brow in her direction. "You're too good for him, Sammi."

"Don't call me that." She shuddered. He'd said the same thing about Robert. And that had ended in tragedy.

"So what's your name, now? Dani, right?" He bounced his right foot for a moment on top of the duffel and pressed his forearm against his side. "Boyfriend said so. Maybe Danielle?"

"Stop." She couldn't reveal anything to this man who deserved none of her trust. "I'll not tell you anything."

"Except where you get off." Tonio grunted as he resettled in his seat and grinned at her.

"You can't come home with me." Her voice rose enough to garner a furrowed brow from the oldest of the girls at the front.

"Very indelicate, you know. Immodest. And I know how important that is to you." He started to drape his arm across the back of the seat. His face twisted, and he halted the movement. A red smudge showed on his white tux shirt before he pulled his arm back down.

"Whose blood is that?" Considering the company the man had kept, she wouldn't put battery or even murder past him.

"It's nothing. Stained from some meat. That *was* a restaurant, you know."

"You weren't working in the kitchen."

He scowled. "Stop being so nosy."

She glanced at the lighted board showing the next stop. Only a few blocks from where she needed to disembark. She had to act. Had to do something.

The bus pulled to a stop, its first since she'd gotten on. The family rose to exit.

A war battled within her. If she used them to distract Tonio, she might earn her escape, but did she dare? Was she willing to place them in such a dangerous position?

Decision made. Again.

"My stop is two away. We should move up."

"No need." He pointed to a lighted circle. "That's what the button is for, right?"

"Look, you can't come with me. I have a roommate." She shoved her purse between them.

"So, you tell her you're not to be disturbed."

"She knows me better than to believe I'd invite you."

He chuckled. "I forgot. Miss Purity."

"Laugh if you want, but it's true. And my roommate knows it." Surely this would stop him. What possible reason could he have for wanting to stay with her?

"Then you're gonna need to find a way to get me in there, toots. You owe me." His sentenced ended in a growl. Or was it a groan?

"How do you get that? I owe you nothing." Knife or gun or whatever, she was getting off of this bus and without him.

He gingerly eased the jacket flap open again. "This blood is mine." He grunted softly as he allowed the jacket to fall back into place. "And it's your fault."

Chapter Five

Jay's stomach lurched. Despite his years of training, had he gotten to eat anything, he'd have lost it. For an instant nothing moved. Jay didn't even breathe. The officer behind him gasped, shaking him back into action. "Call paramedics."

Metal shelves lined the room filled with cardboard boxes, crates, and various meat cuts sealed in plastic. But at least a dozen people, both male and female, littered the floor.

He rushed to the woman nearest him. She lay on her side, her blonde head resting on the shoe of the man next to her. Her heavy makeup stood out on the pallor of her face. Jay pressed his fingertips into her fleshy neck. Her skin was cool to the touch, but a definitive beat throbbed in her carotid artery.

Praise God.

"Get her out of here." He gestured to two officers standing by. "Get her a coat or a tablecloth. Something."

He moved to the man who had cushioned her head with his foot. The man groaned slightly as Jay turned him over.

Another one who was alive. Were all of them that way?

"This guy's only knocked out." Gutierrez and the female officer hoisted a young man in a yellow, short-sleeved button-down and khaki pants. "And I'm hearing there are two other rooms like this one. The cooler next door has customers, and the next one down has staff."

"All alive? Uninjured?"

"Seems that way." He followed the officer who carried the man's feet. "Ambulances in route."

Jay released a long exhale and hoisted the heavy man's shoulders. "Need some help in here."

A pale-faced young officer appeared at the doorway.

"Can you get his feet?"

The cop, a wiry rookie, was stronger than he looked. He lifted the man's legs quickly, almost knocking Jay over.

"Easy does it."

A metal canister thunked on the floor under the man and rolled into the corner.

An electric shock zinged through Jay. "Go!" He practically shoved the kid out of the door. "Get this man outside." He directed another cop to take his place at the shoulders of the still-sleeping customer.

Chances were, that canister was the agent that conked all of the people out. But he wasn't a betting man. Didn't like to rely on chances. "Get those people out of here." Jay pointed to the last few couples in the corner and several uniforms rushed toward them.

He tapped one of the officers on the shoulder. "We need the bomb squad."

The middle-aged beat cop lifted his graying eyebrows and grabbed for the mic attached to his uniform.

Jay shouted instructions to clear the restaurant and picked up a plump-ish woman nearing middle age.

"Don't cha think the can's prolly the thing used t'gas these folks?" The beat cop had completed his call and tugged at the foot of a rather large man.

"Yeah, but do we really want to leave our safety to my assumptions?"

The man grunted. "I see yer point."

Jay laid the woman on a tablecloth alongside other patrons as an ambulance parked at the entrance to the building. He caught an officer exiting without a victim. "Anyone else still in there?"

"Coming out now."

"Stab wound over here." One of the cops flagged a paramedic.

Stabbed? No one had appeared hurt. Jay maneuvered toward the twenty-something man. A black jacket was knotted around his middle. The medic cut off the fabric and then proceeded to snip through the man's sport coat and dress shirt.

Jay narrowed his focus on the discarded material. Where had the jacket come from? Most of the male customers were in sport coats. Not anything like this, though.

He leaned over the paramedic's open case and eyed a box of disposable gloves. Flashing his badge, he pointed at the container. "I'm with the crime scene unit. You mind?"

"G'ahead." The man hardly glanced up from his task.

Jay slipped on a pair and picked up the clothing article from where the medic had tossed it. Even he knew better than to wear black in summer, but this was no informal sports coat. The black collar had a satiny effect. Had to be from a tuxedo.

That meant it belonged to a member of the wait-staff. He crossed to where they had been collected. Nine men in tux coats. No one wore a tuxedo without the coat.

Questions bubbled. How many wait-staff had been on duty? Who gave his coat to the injured man? And since the waiters and cooks were separated from the customers, how had the coat gotten to the man?

For the last one, likely it had happened at the time and place of the stabbing. But he'd not be able to learn more about that until the bomb squad cleared the building.

He hated waiting.

"Is he gonna be all right?" Jay hovered behind the paramedic once again.

"Looks that way." The man moved aside while two EMT's lifted the victim onto a gurney. "Mighta been a different story had someone not thought to create that pressure bandage."

"The coat?"

The sandy-haired medic nodded. "That knot was perfectly positioned to press directly on the puncture. Good thing." He repacked his gear and moved toward the staff members who had begun to groggily move about.

Jay scanned the group stirring. Most in white cook's garb or wearing heavy shoes and blackish pants. He focused on those in black. He'd paid little attention to the waiter who had helped Dani, but he remembered the guy was big and with an Italian ancestry.

The waiter he'd seen wasn't part of this group. Though probably two, maybe three of them were as tall or taller than Jay, they were skinny and one was much older with a goatee.

Jay squatted and laid his hand on one waiter's shoulder. "Can you tell me what happened?"

"Uh… you a cop?" The man's eyes looked glazed.

"Sergeant Hunter. How did you wind up in the

locker?"

The man moved slowly, shaking his salt and pepper head and then putting his hand to it as though to steady his thoughts. "Some men. Masked. In black. One had a gun."

"Where did they come from?"

"The alley. Rushed in. Shoved the cooks and me… and another waiter who came to the kitchen for food… shoved us in the pantry. Before we could plan or react, two more of our waiters and a busboy came in. Then the others and the maître 'd." He rubbed his eyes.

Sounded like it all happened fast. Surely they had security cameras that would hold more of the story. "Did you hear them say anything?"

"Not a word. Somebody tossed in a can that started smokin'. That's it."

The timetable took shape. He and Dani had likely been sitting in the dining room when all of that had happened. "How many waiters did you have tonight?"

"Huh?"

"Waiters. The men in tuxedos? How many?"

"Oh, eight. Always eight." His voice faded.

"And the bald guy." Jay raised his volume and touched the man's shoulder. "Your maître 'd. He makes nine, right?" Which would make all of the tuxedo coats accounted for.

"Yeah... I mean, no." He dropped his chin. "You don't make sense."

"What?" Jay reeled in his frustration and eased off the intensity of his tone. The guy was foggy enough without adding undue stress. "What did I say that didn't make sense to you? Weren't there nine?"

"Nine, all right. But that's our maître 'd." He pointed to a thin man with a full head of silvery hair.

Grime Spree

Chapter Six

"Lean there and don't say anything." Dani gave Tonio a push, hoping the rough wood facing on her complex would keep him vertical.

"What are you planning?" His weak whisper would have been lost had it not been for the echo of the second-floor breezeway. He let the long handle of his duffel fall.

"Shh." She patted his shoulder then turned and unlocked her door, nudging it open. "You here, Tasha?"

"As of a few seconds ago." Her roommate exited the kitchen with a bowl of popcorn. Her white-gold spirals bounced, as always, giving her the impression of perpetual motion. "Study night. My tort prof. is killing me. And I mean literally. I'm so stressed over tomorrow's test, I haven't eaten any real food for days."

That explained the popcorn. "And?"

Tasha held her arms out and posed. "Three and a half pounds. Yea-rah." She popped a kernel into her mouth. "But tonight's key. Mozart on the headphones and everything."

"Heavy." Great. The chances of her hearing Tonio's voice reduced considerably with that detail. "Good luck tomorrow."

"Thanks." She rolled her eyes and pressed the door closed behind her.

Dani crossed to the front entrance and paused for a moment. Did she really dare smuggle a man in here? Especially that man. Her logical mind insisted against it, but she couldn't leave him bleeding on the porch.

She froze when Tasha's voice rose from

behind her door belting, "...defying gravity." So much for Mozart, but better for Dani's purposes.

She cracked the front door open and peeked out.

"Well?" Tonio hissed through a pained expression.

She'd half-hoped he'd moved along, but in his condition, it wasn't likely he could go far.

"You should be at the hospital." Dani reached for him.

"Get that." He pointed to the duffel and gritted his teeth.

For mercy sakes. She looped the long strap over her shoulder then supported him under his left shoulder and wrapped her arm around his waist, grabbing the waistband of his tux pants on his right side. She half-walked, half-dragged the man through the entrance and across to her bedroom. Dropping the bag, she propped him on her bed before she returned to close the front door.

Tasha came out of her room. "I thought the

door closed. My curtains always move."

"Yeah, I thought one of the dogs across the way was whimpering." Dani hated how easy lying had become.

"Nuisance, little yapper." She returned with a small bag of chocolate candy and popped one into her mouth. "Mm, sweet and salty. So you're home sort of early. Didn't things go well?"

She didn't have to fake her consternation on this one. Nor did she have to lie. "Plans change." Though this time not entirely by Jay's hand.

"Again?" She carried her bowl toward Dani and crawled into the oversized recliner. "Honey, I think you need to have a talk with that man."

Dani eyed Tasha's seat. A tiny glance to her right would reveal Tonio reclining on her bed. Why hadn't she closed her door?

God, please don't let Tasha see him.

She stayed where she was, hoping to hold Tasha's attention, leaning against the door and crossing one foot over the other. "It's the new position he's in."

"I know. And before that, it was the possibility of the promotion. After this job is old, he'll simply find something else to distract him."

Dani didn't want to accept that, but after tonight, the likelihood of further dates was slim. "Speaking of distraction, aren't you supposed to be studying?"

"I want to be here for you, roomie."

"If you think I'm going to be responsible for you failing this test, think again." She pushed off the door. "I'm fine and we can talk tomorrow."

"But…."

"But, nothing." Dani snatched the candy bag from her and used it as a lure toward her roommate's room. "Go, go."

"Okay, okay." The blonde followed the bag, taking it from Dani as she retreated. "But I'm here if you…."

Dani pulled the door shut, closing off any chance for Tasha to see Tonio. "Mozart.

Remember?"

Her roommate's muffled, "I remember," sounded downright pathetic.

She hadn't spotted the man in the other room. Thank heaven. Dani raided the first aid cabinet from the linen closet in the hallway and dashed back to Tonio, this time shutting the door with barely a click.

The man leaned back, his head against her turquoise wall and his face slack.

"You still with me, Tonio?" She pressed her fingers against the pulse point on his wrist.

"Yes." His word slurred, but he opened his eyes. "You're not getting rid of me that easy. Not that bad. Tired is all."

She pulled out her sewing shears and prepared to cut through his bloodied shirt.

"Wait, what are you thinking?" He leaned forward and unbuttoned his shirt. "This is Armani."

"And stained beyond repair." She replaced the scissors in her kit and helped him slip off his warm-up jacket and out of the ruined designer-wear.

He grimaced as he shrugged it off of his left shoulder. She tried to look past his physique, still athletic, but not as ripped as she remembered.

Then, she got her first look at the puncture and her stomach roiled. Strange how this affected her. After all, she had no trouble cleaning up after dead bodies—they no longer felt any pain. Dealing with an actual wound was another story. "Good grief, Tonio, what did you do?"

He needed medical attention. Something beyond her eighth-grade Red Cross certification.

Groaning, he leaned back against the wall again and started talking. "The job wasn't supposed to go down like it did."

"How was it supposed to go?" The more he talked, the less he would think about the pain. She pressed a thick pad of gauze onto the wound and used more surgical tape than needed to stick it firmly to his deeply tanned torso.

"…then when the customer was stabbed…."

"What?" She'd only been giving half an ear to his monologue. "Who was hurt?"

"I dunno. But helping him made the boss mad." He explained how the boss had turned the knife on Tonio and left him behind.

Even more, she wanted to take him to a clinic. "What if the blade punctured something important? I mean, it could have nicked an intestine or any number of things."

He shook his head. "A flesh wound."

"You need a doctor."

He leaned closer and grabbed her wrist. "I'm not going to the ER. This is a knife wound. One look, and they'll call in some cop to ask a bunch of questions." He released her. "Wouldn't be such a great thing for you either, now would it?"

That was true. "Well, you can't stay here."

He released her and relaxed with a sad smirk. "Your concern is touching."

"Hey, I treated the wound and patched you up." Her whisper grew too loud, and she brought the volume back down. "I'll even help you pay for a hotel room." She grabbed the wallet out of her purse and dumped the contents out on the edge of the bed. "I've got…" She ruffled through the bills and fingered the change. "… Thirty-five… no, thirty-six, fifty."

"I don't need your money." He held up his hand then let it drop back onto the bed. "Let me have a few minutes. A short nap." He leaned back against the wall, and his face went slack.

She waited for a moment and watched for his eyes to crack open. He'd duped her before with his helpless act. More than once.

But this time, his eyes didn't open. Instead, his breathing deepened and took on the rhythm of sleep.

Really? Now what was she supposed to do? He couldn't stay there, could he? Then again, maybe it was for the best. He could always leave after she and Tasha went to their job site tomorrow.

Circling her bed, she nearly tripped on the

green duffel. She shoved it under her bed and turned the lamp atop the bedside table on. Then, she collected a modest set of pajamas from her bureau before switching off the overhead light. She scooped up her purse and went back into the living room. She'd fallen asleep in front of the TV before, so her sleeping on the couch wouldn't be unnatural.

Her purse vibrated, and she tugged out her silenced phone.

Oh, no. Jay.

Jay had the full story by the time the rest of his team finally arrived. He set the others to work collecting the data and making scans but pulled his longtime partner aside.

Cal directed one of the junior techs tending to blood droplets on a table before he gave Jay his full attention. "What happened to your big date? I thought I took the lake suicide just so you didn't have to cancel on your girl again."

"This was the big date." Jay opened his arms. Then he pointed at the table where he had been seated with Dani. "Or rather that was."

The older man squinted. "You two were here when all of this happened?"

"Not exactly." Jay explained how Dani had gotten some mysterious illness. "She knows something about this. She has to."

"Ask her."

Jay rubbed a finger over his chin. "She's not picking up my calls."

Cal plopped his hand on Jay's shoulder. "That's tough. But I'm still in the dark about this robbery. What? Did some crazies just run in and gas the place?"

Jay had a different idea. "These guys were calculating and well-studied. They knew when to come in and how to take the places of the staff members."

"They switched places. That makes better

sense. With those positions secure, they could shoot the front door bolts and control the customers."

"Exactly." And Dani had known about the robbery beforehand. Otherwise, why the act? But if that was true, he'd have to arrest her. Could he really do that?

Cal ran a hand through his cropped, grayish-blond hair. "This isn't the craziest robbery I've ever heard about, but it gets pretty close."

Jay had to do whatever he could to get Dani to open up to him. And yet, his chest ached at the thought of questioning her. Her attempts at evasion tore into him as though each lie and half-truth that she'd spouted scraped his heart across a lemon zester.

He wasn't sure about anything more than her name at this point. Except that he cared about her. "I need to question her, but I feel like I'm risking our relationship."

"I could do it. She might not even know anything." He tapped the junior-tech's shoulder and pointed out another bit of blood splatter under one of the tables.

"She does. My gut is convinced she does." But was it worth ruining what they might become? "How can I build on what we have when she's not leveling with me?"

"Had an ex-wife like that."

"And look how that ended." Cal had only one ex-wife, but somehow every woe known to man was wrapped up in that woman. Jay shook his head. His partner wasn't helping.

"It was good for a long time though." Cal chuckled. "Mighta even lasted if I'da learned more about this God of yours before I started looking for my entertainment elsewhere."

Their discussions about God and Cal's heart-felt questions had been a blessing. It was a shame Jay couldn't have prompted the topic before Cal's divorce. "I'm sorry, man."

"Not your fault, kid. I wouldn't have listened. You know that. But you listen to me when I tell you to find a way to trust that girl. She cares about you, kid. Better than you deserve. Well, better than *I* deserve anyway." He laughed again.

He was right. Jay had let other matters—like the way Dani avoided his questions yet spoke to his captain—bother him. Could his suspicions be some type of jealousy?

And if that were the case, he needed to release it thoroughly. "Okay. You go out to her place. Go ahead and take her to the station, but let Cap know. He'll want to be in on the questioning."

"You want me to arrest her?"

"No." How could he think such a thing? "But between you and Captain Madison, hopefully you can persuade her to tell you what she's been hiding from me."

"You got it. I'll give you a call when we know something."

Jay turned away and left him to complete the processing. He collected the tuxedo jacket, bagged and labeled, from one of his investigators and made his way to his car. The coat needed to be secured, and his trunk provided a solid spot for it.

As he walked, he dialed Dani's number again. It wasn't that late. He pressed the phone to his ear and listened to a ring. If only he weren't positive that she knew something about the crime. The impression had started out as a light fog but had grown so opaque, it blotted out all other possibilities.

"Hello?" Her voice held a formal tone. Usually, he got a "Hey, Handsome," or at least a "Hey-there."

"I'm finishing up at the restaurant." Maybe if he broached the subject, she'd share her details—something entirely innocent, no doubt.

"Everything all right?"

Her initial question struck him as odd. They'd known the robbery was in the shopping center they'd just come from, but nothing had been said about a restaurant. And there had been several eateries of various styles there. Wouldn't asking about that be her first reaction? Unless she already knew what place had been robbed. "Okay is relative." At least no one had died.

"I see."

No other questions? The woman was practically an amateur detective, always asking for the details of his crime scenes or sharing her observations. A foreboding hit his stomach like a cargo of dead fish. "I'd like to come over for a few minutes."

"Oh, Jay, that's nice. Really nice, but... I... remember? I wasn't feeling well?" Her attempt at diversion fell flat. Her voice pitched unnaturally high. Practically a squeak.

"I'm sorry you're sick, but I need to speak with you."

"We're talking now."

"Dani, I'm serious." He nodded to a man in a light blue hoodie passing by on the sidewalk. "I don't plan to stay long."

"I'm... already on my way to bed."

No way. Not this early.

She coughed. "Whatever this is has totally knocked me out."

Another lie. How would he ever trust her again? But that issue was secondary. She had answers he needed. The realization made him sick. Cal would have to take care of the situation after all.

"All right, I won't come. I'm disappointed in the way this has turned out."

"Me, too." Strength in her tone seemed to return rather suddenly. "But I understand. You have a job to do."

She didn't understand his meaning at all.

"I liked the place though." Her voice warmed. She didn't sound the slightest bit sick. "Bella Noda? The Beautiful Knot? Maybe we can try to go there again?"

What chance was there of that? "I'll talk to you soon." He ended the call.

She was in Cal's hands now.

He reached his car. The blue hoodie guy lingered at a white sports car beside him.

He unlocked his door and gave the man a tight-lipped smile. "Sorry if I blocked you in." He tossed the bagged coat onto his passenger seat and showed his badge from his back pocket.

"No problem." The man's voice had a laid-back tone.

Good. Jay didn't need the new complication of an argument with an uptight urbanite. He climbed into the driver's seat.

"I could use a ride." The man appeared at Jay's open door with a weird smile on his flat lips. "If you don't mind." He lifted a thirty-eight with a silencer attached.

Chapter Seven

Succeeding in getting past Jay's insistence, Dani made a grilled cheese and munched on it and a salad while watching a rerun on TV. A murder mystery, of course.

She tugged at her dress. Maybe she should have changed into those pajamas. They were perfectly modest, but they were still pajamas. She couldn't bring herself to justify wearing them with a man under her roof.

Blue jeans—or better, running shorts and a tee shirt—would give her comfort without making her feel awkward. She cracked her door open, expecting to tiptoe inside to get the needed clothes.

But Tonio was awake. He leaned back in the same way in which she'd left him, but with her Bible in his lap. "I always knew you were sorta religious. Didn't figure on this."

"What are you talking about?" She glanced at Tasha's door. A dim light shown under the wood. Her roommate was probably still studying. She pushed her door closed and leaned against it.

"This." He pointed to a page where she'd written things in the margin. "You wrote about real situations. About Robert?"

She put a cool hand to her cheek. How dare he read through her personal notes. Taking a breath, she tried to focus on the opportunity. "When I read God's Word, sometimes He shows me truth that needs to be applied to my life." Not that Tonio would understand all of that.

"Like this part where you underlined the 'sending you out as sheep in the midst of wolves.' Am I one of those wolves, Sammi?"

Shutting her eyes, she lifted a prayer for the right words. "I underlined that after I found out about things. And I failed all of you. You... Robert." She moved toward him and turned a few pages earlier in the book of Matthew. "Here. I'm supposed to shine my light." She pointed to verse 5:15. "But I didn't. I didn't want any of you to think I was odd, so I kept my faith to myself for the most part."

"So all of this means something to you? Like God's real and all."

"Oh, yes." Her answer came without hesitation, like an exhale. "Not only is He real, but He loves me like a Father, helping me walk through hard times and giving me the promise that things will work out for my ultimate good."

"That's why you weren't so scared of me earlier."

Hmm. She hadn't been scared. Startled, but not panicking. "I guess so. I mean, what's the worst thing you could have done to me?"

"I coulda killed you. I wouldn't have, just so's you know. But I coulda." He kept his eyes trained on the book in his lap and turned a page.

"And that would have catapulted me into the presence of my Heavenly Father—into the glories of heaven itself with no more sorrow or sickness or worry or fear." She cocked an eyebrow at him. "Why should that scare me?"

"That's twisted." He glanced up at her with a half-smile.

"Not that I want to die. I don't. More than anything, I want to testify at that trial. I want..." She couldn't put the whole truth into words without tears spilling. "I want justice." She pointed to the book. "But this love letter from God gives me hope and promises that this life is only the beginning for me."

His smirk dropped off. "I'm glad for you, Sammi-girl. You always were good."

"No. I wasn't." She wrapped her left arm around her back and clasped her right elbow. "God doesn't save me because I'm good. He saves me because He's good. See, God made people to be His friends, His companions. But He's perfect, so He can't be around us, because we're bad. Even a little bad is filthy. But He worked out a solution." She leaned over again and swiped at the pages, stopping in Romans. "This book explains who we are to God and what He did for us."

His gaze rested on the page, then rose back to her. "Bad is one thing. I'm on a whole new level."

"Read this."

"You really believe all-a-this."

"Absolutely." She straightened. "Truth is truth, whether you believe it or not."

"And this is truth?" He moved the book so that the page became more fully illuminated.

"Read it. Find out for yourself." She slipped out of the door and closed it behind her, breathing out a prayer that Tonio would indeed find truth in the pages of God's Word.

A light tap at the front door froze her. Had

Tonio called some of his associates? Or maybe Jay had changed his mind and had come over anyway? She glanced toward Tasha's room. Finally, her light was off.

Another tap jolted Dani. She had to open it before Tasha awakened, but to what? Or more importantly, to whom?

Jay stared at the weapon for a solid second before lifting his eyes back to the man's face.

"Maybe you should simply concentrate on your steering wheel. A vehicle such as this one can be very dangerous, don't you think?" The man gave a creepy laugh and popped the automatic lock with one hand while the muzzle of the gun butted against the base of Jay's head.

What did this man want? "A car's not worth my life. Yours either. You're welcome to mine."

He laughed again, like a short blast from a

machine gun or a fifth-grade bully. "Thanks. No. But put your hands on the roof-liner."

Jay slowly lifted his hands. His own weapon, tucked into his holster under his jacket, seemed miles away. Not like he had any type of shot even if he could reach it. He pressed his palms on the fabric. "If you don't want the car, then what do you want?"

"Just a ride, Officer." He'd opened the back door and climbed inside before Jay could make a one-count. The gun shoved against the back of his head, now.

Jay ran through any defensive moves he could make. Not that his position with the crime scene team called for much of that. Even on his best day, he'd get a bullet in his brain before he so much as bruised the hooded guy behind him.

"Now, keep that left hand on the roof there and start your engine with your right."

Jay started to move.

"And be very careful that you follow my

instructions. K?"

His voice sounded like that used by an always-smiling sales rep. Still, Jay did as he was told, then, again following directions, rested one hand on the gearshift and the other on the steering wheel.

The gun moved to his right side. The guy gave him instructions on which direction to turn on his way out of the parking lot.

"Where are we going."

"What can I say, Officer? I like to joyride."

"Is that what this is?" If only he could find out what the man was after.

His passenger moved to the other side of the back seat and leaned away for a moment. "Something like that." The sound of a seatbelt clicked.

Before Jay could act on the man's distance, the gun again pushed into his ribcage. "Take a left over there."

The area was full of light industrial buildings and small, non-retail businesses. "I still don't know what you want." If only Jay could put on his seatbelt, he could ram the car into something, but at this point, doing that could kill him and not hurt his hooded friend at all.

"Right at that stop sign."

Jay made the turn. The plastic-wrapped jacket in the seat next to him slid in his direction. That was it. He could use that bundle to distract the man. It just needed to slip a little closer to him.

The man kept his gun trained but pulled out his cell phone. "Another right at this street."

No stop sign here. Jay took the curve a little faster than he normally would, but it gave enough inertia to slide the bag even more toward him. Just what he needed.

"Now." The word came from behind him exactly when Jay moved to grab the plastic bag. The guy leaned back against his seat as Jay tossed the bag in his direction. He pulled on the door latch to jump out, but his eye caught a view of the grill of a Mack truck.

Just before the world exploded.

Chapter Eight

Dani breathed out relief when she saw Cal on her front porch instead of Jay. "Didn't I talk to your partner a while back?"

"Yep." He didn't smile. Simply stood there with his khaki-clad legs about shoulder-width apart and the thumb of one hand hanging from one of his belt loops.

She stepped onto the porch, her feet instantly cooled by the cement, and pulled the door closed behind her. "So I'll say the same to you as I did to him. I'm not feeling well. And I'm on my way to bed."

"Dressed like that?"

Maybe she should've done the pajama bit after all. She tugged at the fabric bunching above the belted middle and lowered the hemline of her skirt. "Yes. Why don't you go call your friend and tell him that I'll think about all of this tomorrow?" Wasn't that a line from some old movie?

"Sorry about this." He raised his other hand, and his wallet fell open to reveal his badge.

"Am I under arrest?" Her mouth dropped open. If Tonio had gotten her into that much trouble, he'd be sorrier than he was now.

"No. Not yet. I'm hoping we can avoid that."

"Is this some twisted way that Jay's getting back at me?" No. As soon as she said it, she regretted the words. The man didn't have a devious bone in his body.

"You should know better than that." His scowl matched the one she felt. "Maybe you aren't as good for him as I thought you were. Either way, Captain Madison is waiting at the department to speak to you. Do you need to change?"

He turned the knob of her door and pushed it open for her.

She stepped inside. "Uh… no. No, I'm quite comfortable."

He remained where he'd been, a few inches outside the door facing. "Except for shoes." He pointed to her bare feet.

Which were in her room, next to the bed where Tonio sat reading her Bible. Not an option. She eyed Tasha's wedge slip-ons placed next to the couch where she'd discarded them. "I'll wear these." She clamped her jaw shut and tried not to look at her closed bedroom door. Determined to stuff her feet into shoes at least a full size smaller than she liked, she made a silent promise to get Tasha another pair. Thankfully, they were made for comfort, though the small size pinched and cramped her toes.

Remaining silent during the ride took every ounce of will power she possessed. Cal was Jay's number one fan, apparently. Couldn't stop telling about his exploits and how the man deserved her trust.

He was all of those things. And her heart knew that, but she could trust no one. And besides, telling Jay her secrets had little to do with her faith in the man. Her silence was more about the conviction of what would happen to him if certain people found out that he knew.

She'd already risked her safety about as far as Matthew was willing to go by talking to the police captain. He'd mentioned moving her right away. Some place like the frozen north where she could put her social life on hold for the next six months, but she'd refused. Of course, he hadn't been that serious. More trouble for him if she had to be relocated.

But as much as she hated secrets and lying, especially to Jay, telling him the truth was out of the question. Besides the danger, he'd hate her if he ever found out all that she'd done.

So admitting anything to his partner was out of the question.

Yet he accompanied her into Madison's office and stood in the corner when she sat in the open chair in front of the desk.

Madison ignored his presence and put his full attention on her. "Hunter seems to think you know something about the night's restaurant robbery." The captain leaned against his desk with his arms crossed, looking rather buzzard-like.

She glanced at Cal. "Discretion is rather important, don't you think?"

"I think Hunter is one of my best officers, and keeping him in the dark is frustrating the tar out of him, or don't you think he can tell?"

He knew she'd been hiding something? "I didn't realize."

"Well, you should have. Cal, here, can do a little diversion if need be. I've already spoken to Donaldson about it. It's either this or he simply moves you again."

Madison had talked with Matthew behind her back? "I'd like to hear that from Matthew himself."

"Sure. However, there is a third option. We may see fit to stick you in a cell in the back wing."

"You can't arrest me." Could he? That would make her identity precarious at best.

"I can, and I will, unless you have the answers I need."

She stiffened. Obviously, he thought he could intimidate her into spilling her guts. And it was working. "I think I should contact my Witness Protection agent before I say anymore." She looked at the ecru toes of her borrowed shoes. Fine. Now Cal knew. It was only a matter of time before he told his buddy.

"Witness…." Cal's whisper breathed out as Madison circled the desk. "That clears up a few things."

The captain punched a few buttons on his phone. He had Matthew's number programmed? She hadn't been in trouble that many times had she?

She sorted through the events… maybe she had.

"Agent Donaldson? Tom Madison, DPD. Do you have a moment?" He glanced at Dani. "Yes, sir, I'm afraid she's rather unwilling to discuss matters."

Matthew's voice sounded like a chipmunk through the receiver. A loud chipmunk.

"I thought perhaps you could persuade her."

Regardless of the captain's threats or his bullying tactics, she wouldn't reveal what she knew about the restaurant situation. She couldn't even tell Matthew about Tonio. He'd pull her out within the hour. This wasn't going to end well.

"Fine. I'll put you on speaker." He fumbled with the old-fashioned cord for a moment, then it clicked into place. The captain pointed to Dani.

"Hello, Matthew."

"What did you do now?" Of all of Matthew's clients, Dani must've been his biggest headache. At least he sounded like he had one every time she spoke to him.

"I didn't *do* anything. I simply happened to be near the scene of a robbery." And that was indeed the truth of it.

"Then why am I wasting my time speaking with you?"

A sarcastic retort poised on her tongue, but she sucked it back inside. "The fact is, I left the scene... prior to the robbery."

"Prior to the... okay, Dani, what are you not telling me?"

"I didn't know what was going to happen...." Okay, she'd let them know some of the story. "...but I felt pretty sure something was about to." Still, she couldn't say who she saw, or Tonio's mugshot would be posted all over Dallas.

"And how did you divine this truth? Do you now have some sort of prophetic ESP?"

Dani's lips pressed together. Matthew's biting sarcasm did nothing for her already salty disposition. She glanced up at Cal. He stared hard at her. Bet this changed his mind about her for good. "I saw someone I knew. Someone who used to be with Robert."

"A name?" The captain sat forward.

"Who?" Matthew's voice deepened.

"I... didn't know him very well." Not *very* well.

"But did he recognize you?" Matthew's urgency reminded her of what she had at stake. If he thought she'd been compromised....

"I'm still okay here, Matthew." She focused again on the story. "But I had the feeling I needed to leave. Needed to go quick, so I pretended to be sick to convince Jay to take me home."

The captain sat back and began writing. "You think the man you saw might have been involved in the robbery?"

She let the emotion drain from her face. "I know his former occupation as a crook, but I have no way of knowing anything else." Except that Tonio had flat-out told her about the situation.

"And you don't know the man's name." The

captain stabbing her would have felt better.

Diversion time. "I know very little about the man except that he was part of my old life."

"And he didn't recognize you." Matthew's comment made the captain's question pale.

"He looked right at me. I think I would notice a glimmer of recognition." There. She hadn't exactly lied. She *would* have noticed. She *did* notice.

"Good, because I'd hate to go through all the trouble to move you. I already spend more time on you than—"

"Any of your other security clients. I know." Yet Matthew still felt the need to tell her at every opportunity.

"So what was this man doing at the restaurant?" The captain laid down his pen and clasped his fingers together on his desk top.

"I guess he was a waiter. He was pouring water. Acting like the other waiters."

The captain's brows furrowed. "So you only

saw him pouring water."

"He seemed to scan the room." She fidgeted in her seat. "I pretended that I needed to go to the bathroom when I saw him."

"And you didn't see him again?" This from Matthew.

She studied the Mason jar full of dull pencils and a few pens. If she told Matthew the truth, she'd not have to worry about meeting Jay's family on the fourth of July. She might not even lay eyes on the man again.

Though with the way she'd been so dishonest with him, that was a real possibility anyway.

"I simply made my way to the back door and asked someone to go tell my date that I was there."

"Another waiter?" The captain scratched a note. He and Cal traded looks. Had she said something wrong?

"Y-yes." She didn't need to go any deeper there.

"What did he look like?" Madison pulled a

form out of a tray on his desk and began filling the boxes with notes.

"I don't know. I was a little nervous. Didn't pay attention."

"Tall, short, dark, light, brunette, blond? Anything?"

"It was a guy." She couldn't make someone up. Not on the spot like this. "Waiters all look alike to me. Wore a white shirts, black pants."

Cal scowled. He didn't buy it. Jay had probably told him about her habit of noticing details. Especially things that weren't straight or in place. Like the third button on Cal's shirt. He'd obviously had to sew it back on it but had reconnected it a tiny bit higher than it was supposed to be.

"But you recognized the one you'd known before." Jay's superior lifted his left eyebrow a millimeter. Oh, great. He wasn't buying her story, either.

"He... well, yes. I mean. The guy resembled

the one I'd known before. Maybe I made a mistake."

He pulled out another sheet of paper. "So what did *he* look like?"

Dani swallowed. Even without a name, Tonio would stand out in Matthew's mind. And once he figured it out, he'd know that Dani had been lying. "Um. Sort of tall… ish… dark… ish."

"African American?" Madison wrote a note.

"No, deeply tanned."

"Hispanic?"

"I don't think so." Italian. Very. But she wasn't going to hand that over. "Clean-shaven." At least that didn't point to Tonio anymore than any of the other men who had been around. Well, most of the other men. There had been a few uber-bearded shaggy fellows, but they never stuck around long. Looked too out of place in that starched world.

"And his build?"

A hulk. Matthew would recognize him in an instant. "I couldn't really say." Really. Couldn't.

Say.

"Your description fits a dozen known associates involved in the ring. Most are still at large." Matthew sounded exasperated.

"I can't help that." And she wouldn't help the agency prosecute Tonio. Not after all that he'd done for her. Before and now.

Captain Madison glanced at his notes. "So you're telling me that you recognized a man from your past. That's why you wouldn't tell Hunter anything. But you can only barely describe this guy, don't know his name, had no idea what he was doing there except pouring water, and didn't know that the place was about to be robbed."

"That's the nutshell version, yeah." She released a deep breath. There was no reason for either of them to think she had more to add. Surely they'd let her go.

"All right, Cutter."

Cal's bloodhound cheeks held the faintest tinge of pink.

"Accompany her to interrogation room three, please." Madison pointed to her.

Wait. What? "Why? I've told you what I know."

The captain turned an icy gaze on her. "Excuse me a moment, Miss Foster."

Cal took her elbow and urged her out the door.

"What is the matter with your captain?" How had she tripped up?

"He has this aversion to the lies and half-truths that some people think they can spin."

"Are you calling me a liar?" Her huff seeped out unexpectedly. Of course he was. And unfortunately, he wasn't mistaken.

He barely glanced at her and emitted a mirthless chuckle.

She paused and made him stop. "How's Jay?"

Cal looked the direction in which they'd come. "Mad. Hurt. Helpless. And pretty much everything in between. I hope you'll decide to stay away from him after all of this. Unless you really do get tossed in the can."

"You're not serious." Would they go that far?

"I'm always serious about Jay. And if you can't figure out how to be honest, lady, you need to leave that man be."

Chapter Nine

A metallic taste coated Jay's mouth. Why was he in such a funky position? His pillow had deadened his right ear and his left knee was under his elbow?

He moved his arm, and pain shot down his spine and screamed into his head. His eyes popped open, but he could see nothing. Not even his alarm clock that should be on the table next to him.

"Hey, mister. Ya all right?"

The darkness faded a little, and a blurred image moved near his head. He tried to call out, but something didn't work with his mouth. His jaw wouldn't move.

"I done called an ambulance."

Ambulance… the guy in his car. He looked across to what was left of the driver's side of his Charger. The steering wheel was broken. His hand would have been there if he hadn't been attempting escape. He flexed his fingers. Stiff, painful, but all moving. That didn't declare he hadn't broken something somewhere, but their moving was definitely a good thing.

The guy outside his passenger door kept moving and talking. "I didn't see nothin', but I sure heard it. Came runnin' from up yonder."

Jay concentrated on moving his toes without causing more pain.

"Guy jumped outta your back seat. Thought he was gonna chew out the truck driver, but he jes climbed on up into the cab and rode off with him."

Blue hoodie. The Mack truck. It was coming back to him in flashes, whirling with the approaching sirens. What was this about?

"Hunter?" The voice of Officer Ruidosa approached as the sirens died out. "Hunter you with me, man?"

Jay grunted.

"What happened here?" The back door opened.

"I saw a big ole truck cab, and it drove off as I got here." That man deserved a medal for sticking around. "I work over a block. Night watchman. Was tourin' the perimeter when I heard the crash. Came a'runnin'."

"Good man." Ruidosa crawled into the back seat. "Hunter, you with me?"

I'm with you. Nothing but another grunt.

"Okay, be still. Ambulance will be here in a sec. Looks like you busted your jaw."

He'd sure busted more than his jaw if his pain was any indication. Another siren neared and shut off almost immediately.

"Officer down." Ruidosa called the address in to one of the night dispatch. "Radio the captain and tell Cal."

Finally back at her apartment, Dani slipped her roommate's shoes off and aligned them next to the door while she stretched and curled her toes. Her shoulders ached, probably from stress. How she hated lying. But at least, she'd been allowed to leave. Surely, that meant they finally believed her, right?

Loud knocking on their door startled her. She hoped it had not awakened Tasha. The poor girl needed her sleep. Dani opened it a crack.

Cal stood with both thumbs hooked through belt loops.

"Why are you back?"

"Thought you'd want to know." He stayed on the porch and lowered his voice.

What could he possibly want now? Had they decided to haul her off to jail? Fresh from the grueling hours in the interrogation room with Cal and the captain, she'd thought she'd finally convinced them both that she didn't have anything to do with the robbery and couldn't tell them any more about the man she'd seen.

And she wasn't about to let Cal inside with Tonio probably still sleeping only a few feet away. "Didn't you get all of the information you could possibly need? And more than you should know, considering you're Jay's partner. Your captain did remind you that you can't tell him any of this."

"It's about Jay."

"You didn't tell him anything." Surely not. He'd not had time to betray her confidence in the two minutes it had taken her to get through her front door. "Tell me you didn't do that. That would not only destroy any chance of our relationship, it would likely put him in danger."

He stiffened and glared at her. "He's already in danger. Officer Hunter is down. Got the call as I was pulling out of your lot."

A frigid wave rolled over her. "What?" Down?

"Apparent victim of a car-jacking."

Victim? "Is he…." He had to be okay.

"I only know that he survived the crash. Dispatch sent me the call from an officer on the scene. I'm heading to the hospital, but since I was here, I thought you'd want to know." He stepped back.

She glanced at the closed-off entrance to her bedroom. Did Tonio know anything about this? "Can I go with you?"

Cal hesitated, lingering on the first step.

"Please, I have to see if he's all right. Even if we are never able to repair our relationship, I have to know."

He nodded. "I'll wait for you downstairs."

She watched him descend a moment before closing her door.

Tonio had better *not* know anything about this, or she'd turn him in right here and now. She shoved into her room. "You have some explaining to…." Her hushed voice faded as her empty bed stared at her.

She peeked under the light tan bed skirt. Nothing. She pulled the closet doors open and rifled through her hanging clothes, knocking out a few racks. The clutter would wait. Switching to jeans and a tee shirt, she slipped her feet into her own flats. Then scanning the room, she snatched up her purse and darted for the front door.

Wherever Tonio had gone, he'd taken her Bible with him. Hope swelled, but only for an instant as she sprinted down her stairs. Surely, he didn't have anything to do with Jay's accident.

Please God, let Jay be all right.

He'd have done such and worse in the past, but she didn't want to think that. Not after their discussion. Not to someone who was obviously important to Dani. But even if he would, his injury would have prevented him from doing much of anything.

Except leave. Maybe he hadn't been as hurt as she thought?

She jogged to Cal's cruiser and slipped into the passenger seat. "What hospital?"

"Baylor downtown. They've mentioned a Care Flight. Not sure if they're going that route, but if they're talking about it...."

"It's bad." She swallowed hard and belted herself in as Cal pulled into the street and switched his siren on. "Do you have a recorder thingy in this rig?"

"Like a dash camera?" He glanced at her. His bushy, gray-brown brows formed a uni-brow over a deep crevice.

"I have another statement I need to make." She hated throwing Tonio over, but if someone really attacked Jay, they needed to track down every lead. Including the one that had napped in her bedroom.

He did a double-take. "Thought you were gonna stick to your fairy tale."

"You knew I was lying?"

"We all did."

"So I *did* make mistakes. I thought I'd covered

all of the details."

He growled. "Your biggest mistake was lying in the first place. You weren't giving it up, and the captain's hands were tied because of that WIT-SEC agent of yours." He veered slightly to move around a pickup. "You know that Jay resents the guy because you call him with your problems and don't tell Jay anything."

"He told you that?"

"I wish you'd find a way to trust that man." He flipped a switch on the dash. "Go ahead."

"Okay. My name is Dani Foster. Well, that's my current name. This is for Captain Madison only. I was lying earlier when I said I didn't know the man who recognized me. I couldn't explain it to you because I knew if Matthew Donaldson heard about it, he'd relocate me, and I don't want to leave Dallas. But the man's name is Tonio Ventinelli. He's got a record, so you don't need my description." She paused and held onto a loop on the door when Cal made a sharp right turn heading for downtown.

"But you do need to know that he helped me escape because someone else in the restaurant would have recognized me if he had seen me. I don't know who. Tonio went back and convinced Jay that I was sick, and we left. Then, when Jay dropped me off at the bus stop, so he could go back to the robbery scene, Tonio arrived. He…." What good would it do to tell that Tonio had been hiding in her apartment? Or that he'd been there at all? "He sat with me on the bus and told me about the robbery."

"Out of the air, he sat and chatted with you?" Cal tilted his head. "Aw, Miss Foster, I only look like I'm stupid. Helps me sniff out all sorts of details."

"Well, he seemed to be scared. Maybe he thought being a couple would keep him from being noticed if he was trying to avoid someone." Coming up with new stories was getting way too easy. "That was at first. Then I realized he'd been stabbed."

"How did you know that?" Cal never took his eyes off the road ahead.

"He was wearing a light-weight jacket that slipped open, and I saw the blood on his dress shirt."

"Jacket. But not a tux coat."

"No, a warm-up jacket. Like a windbreaker." She shut her eyes. *That* had been her mistake. "The waiters were all in tuxedos."

"That was one of your errors."

She focused back on Tonio. Her stomach gurgled, more from her revulsion at remembering the wound than from hunger at missing dinner. "Anyway, I helped him as best I could."

Cal jerked up the radio speaker. "Where'd he go?"

She shook her head. "I have no idea. He insisted it was flesh wound."

He replaced the microphone on the speaker.

"We talked for some time, though. He was

afraid the guy in charge would find him."

"Who was that?"

"I never found out, but he'd hurt one of the customers."

"Knifed the guy. We found what I guess was Tonio's tuxedo jacket on him."

She sucked in a quick breath. "Is he going to live?"

"Last I heard, it looked good for him." Cal slowed as the street narrowed for construction. "What can you tell me about that?"

"Tonio only said that he helped him. He'd had some first aid training and tried to get the bleeding to stop. The boss ended up stabbing Tonio when he learned about his doctoring."

"Or learned that he'd left his tux coat behind. Dry cleaner marks." Cal jerked his head toward her then quickly back to the road. "Jay had that coat with him in his car." The hospital loomed high ahead of them. "I wish you'da told us this all earlier."

Me, too. "I had no idea I was putting Jay in danger. I thought I was helping things."

He pulled into a spot near the emergency room doors. "I didn't say you put him in danger. All of this gives more questions than answers. I can't imagine that your new evidence would have made a difference in any of this."

For all of his gruffness, she appreciated Cal's attempt to encourage her. He led the way through the doors to the waiting room where they intercepted another officer that Cal knew.

"Any news?"

"He made it here. And that's good." The man glanced at Dani.

"Dani Foster, Officer Ruidosa." Cal nodded in her direction. "She's Jay's girlfriend."

He lifted his chin in a greeting. "Sorry to meet you under such circumstances."

"Did you get to talk with Jay?" She had to know that Tonio hadn't been involved in hurting him.

"Looked like his jaw was broke. He whispered something that sounded like hoodie... maybe Houdini. Other than that, just grunts."

Houdini? Escape artist? Magician? What in the world did that mean?

Cal put his hand on the other man's shoulder. "Hunter had some evidence. A tuxedo jacket. Bagged and labeled. Find anything like that in the car?"

"You're not the only one who asked. Lieutenant Gates also had that question, but there was no evidence bag and no tuxedo, coat or anything else." He nodded. "Best guess is that coat might have been the purpose of the car-jacking."

Then she had been responsible for his accident. Partly anyway. All of the air left her lungs and an ache built up within the empty vacuum. "Can we see him?" She could hardly choke out the words.

"He's in surgery. Paramedics said there were internal injuries. That's why they Care-Flighted him here." Ruidosa nodded at her then stepped away.

"That coat."

"Yeah." Cal put his hand at her elbow and directed her toward a chair.

"I should have told you all everything from the beginning."

Cal sat catty-corner to her with a groan. "Yes. You should have. Secrets only fool you into believing you're okay when you're really barely hanging onto a cliff. You have to trust the people around you, the ones who have proven they care about you, to help you up."

She shut her eyes. She did trust Jay. With her life... but not with her heart. The moment she began to reveal... images of her past life flashed through her mind. Awful. *Oh. No, no, no.*

"You don't understand." A tear trickled down her cheek.

"Probably not." He moved to extract a folded handkerchief from his front pocket and handed it to her. "Look, you can't go on blaming yourself. And nothing you can do, now, will fix this." He settled into his seat with his elbows propped up on the arms of the chair. "But you can make a change going forward. You need to let the whole truth keep coming out."

Whole truth? No one had seen any of that, yet.

Chapter Ten

Jay emerged from the shadowy alley just in time to see Dani jog away from him down a darkened street. "Wait. You don't know what's out there."

At least, he didn't. She might, with all of her secrets and lies. He felt rather than heard the giant train roaring along the tracks. Wait. Trains? She didn't have any tracks near her place. Where were they? And why was Dani just standing there, watching the train rush toward her?

"Move."

She only looked at him. "I'm sorry."

He jerked. Pain shot through his ribcage.

"Whoa there, kid. Doc says you have to take it easy." Cal's voice connected to the fuzzy image along the wall in front of him. Dim light filtered in from some fixtures behind his head.

"Where?" *Ow.* Something destructive hammered against his mouth. He had to have lost a chunk of his lips and several teeth with that one word.

"You're in the hospital. Do you remember the accident?" Cal's voice and the fuzzy blur moved closer and gained color. "After you left Bella Noda?"

He grunted and tried to nod. "What's wrong with me?" He could do no better than to whisper words through his gritted teeth.

"You are one lucky cuss, kid. Makes me think there's more to this Christian thing you've got going on that I gave you credit for."

Jay sighed. *Don't make me repeat my question, Cutter.*

"Doc says you didn't break your jaw. You only dislocated it. He's put it back into place, but you'll have to have it wired for a couple of days to make sure it stays."

"And?"

"And you're not supposed to talk. I'm to keep you as quiet as possible."

Jay blinked, twice.

"Oh, a couple of busted ribs, minor concussion. A little internal bleeding, but they tied that all up. You didn't break anything else, but you're left side is all bruised up. 'Specially your ankle. Doc says it's remarkable since you weren't even wearing your safety belt."

Good. He'd be able to write even if he couldn't talk, though lifting his hand to gesture for a pen took about all his strength.

"Chill, kid. You're on big-time pain killers. Think of the last filling you had to have at the dentist and compile that deadening all over your body. Sluggish doesn't begin to describe you."

Lovely. *Now give me a pen.* He made the motion again.

"Okay, but it's not like anyone will be able to read your chicken scratch." Cal laid a tablet on his lap and handed him a pen.

D-a-n-i-? Had she had any trouble from the thieves? Had Cal even told her about the accident? What had he learned when he questioned her?

"She's here." Cal came closer and lowered his voice. "Been here all night. She really cares about you, kid. Go easy on her."

Jay breathed a heavy exhale. She'd been there all night? Worried over him? He didn't know how he'd get past her secrecy, but he had to try.

"Before she gets back in here, you need to know a few things."

Yeah, like what she had to do with the robbery and why she couldn't explain things to him.

"She's got reasons for her silence over things. You don't need to question them. She didn't have anything to do with the robbery, though she did recognize one of the thieves. Don't ask how. The captain has put out a bulletin for Tonio Ventinelli. When we get him, I'll give you a full report."

Wait. "How…." How did Dani know a crook?

"Dani finally spilled when she found out about your accident. I think she thought she was protecting you or something."

From what? "How did she know?"

"No talking, remember?" Cal glanced at the closed door. "And I told you not to ask about that. I'm not keen on keeping things from my partner, but you're going to have to trust me that this is one tidbit that isn't going to do you or anyone else any good in knowing."

"But…."

"Trust. Isn't that the thing you've been telling me about? Your faith in Jesus? You simply have to trust that everything He said was true?"

Jay could do nothing but nod. Though having a theological lesson from Cal made the world tilt just a little.

"Yeah. You said you have to pray about things, read the Bible, and then act in the way you think God's telling you. Though I still don't get all of the urging that you talked about."

He would. If Jay could persuade him to submit to the Lord, he'd understand about the way the Spirit urged His people.

"If all that's true, then you've already prayed about Dani. Right?"

Jay stared into the older man's eyes. Here was his best opportunity to share the Gospel with Cal so far. Not only couldn't Jay speak, he couldn't even answer his question truthfully. No. He'd been avoiding that since he got the feeling that Dani was keeping things from him. He shook his head slightly.

"If she's so all-fired important to you, then why haven't you prayed about her? Prayed about the two of you? Prayed about figuring out a way to trust her, 'cause you need to trust her."

Jay tapped the pad and wrote. *I'm afraid God*

will say no. How could he explain this to Cal? He didn't even completely understand it himself.

"Oh, so if you don't pray about it, then you don't have to pay attention to the answer God gives you. That it? If you don't ask permission, you don't have to obey?"

Groan. He should have known that Cal, with his unique knowledge of people, would make a connection that Jay couldn't ignore.

He let his eyes shut. *Oh, God. I'm sorry I didn't trust you with Dani. With our relationship. I pray that You approve, but if You don't, please make it clear to me.*

But hadn't He already been doing that? Showing clearly that He didn't approve? And with every new secret she seemed to keep or question that she avoided, the feelings that Jay should release her built.

Could he let her go?

Dani spotted a single-cup coffee pot in one of the waiting rooms as she took a walking tour to get her blood circulating. "Is this for people who are visiting patients?"

"You bet, honey. You just need to buy the flavor cap there in the machine." The woman pointed to a miniature snack machine filled with an assortment of flavors. "Then have at."

Exactly what she needed. Dani made a large cup of vanilla hazelnut and sipped it as she strolled through a rounded room on the first floor of the Truett building where several hallways came together. Lighted glass shelves filled with bronze hand casts lined the walls. She examined several nameplates and pictures. Dr. Seuss, Charles M. Schultz, Louis Armstrong, Winston Churchill, Walt Disney. Impressive collection.

And examining each of them kept her mind off of Jay. For a while. Until she reached the end of the exhibit.

She tossed her empty cup into a trash container and meandered back the way she'd come.

Would he want to see her? Or did he hate her? If Cal and Madison hadn't believed her stories, then Jay likely didn't trust her either. And why should he?

She couldn't tell him the truth about who she was—all that was in her past. Their relationship would be long gone if that ever happened. But if she went through with the trial—if the convictions were finally achieved—wouldn't that redeem her? Would she be able to release her own guilt?

No. Her responsibility for all that happened would never be gone. And she didn't deserve to get rid of it. She deserved to live with that weight for the rest of her life. Even if it meant that she and Jay would never be together.

Oh, God, please let Jay forgive me, somehow.

She reached his door and tapped. He'd probably still be sleeping, though the doctor said he'd awaken anytime. And once he did, if things still looked as good as they had when he had come from surgery, he'd be able to go home sooner rather than later.

"C'mon in." Cal's voice virtually boomed. Was he attempting to wake Jay up or scare half the floor?

She peeked in. Jay's bed had been raised. His eyes brightened when he saw her. Or had she only imagined that?

He reached out his hand. Rushing forward, she took it and kissed his brow. "I'm so sorry."

"'S'okay, honey." His husky whisper smoothed away a layer of guilt.

"Aannt. No talking." Cal made for the door but paused and pointed at them. "I mean it."

She stroked his short black hair. "The doctor said you might get to go home tomorrow. Maybe even today if things still look good."

He tapped the pad and wrote. *You okay?*

"I'm feeling guilty that we fought last night."

I'm sorry, too. I'm trying to trust you.

How she hated the secrets that were required of her. Her mouth flattened. "You don't have any good reason to trust me, Jay. I know that." A tear vaulted off her bottom lashes and tracked down her cheek.

He lifted his hand and spread the tear into her hairline.

"I wouldn't blame you if you walked away."

With his other hand he gestured to his hospital bed with a smirk on his face.

She released a nervous chuckle. "Well, when you get permission to walk again."

He released her and wrote again. *I care about you. You know that.*

Shutting her eyes, she let her forehead lower to his and rest there a moment. *God, please heal this man, thoroughly. Like I prayed all night. And if he's not the man for me, bring him such joy that he has no doubt of Your guidance.*

"I care about you, too. More than I ever thought possible." She breathed in his musky scent and stepped back. "I knew one of the men at the restaurant last night. Someone I didn't want to see. Never wanted to see again. I can't explain it, but that's why I had to leave."

He watched her, his eyes drooping a little in the corners as he wrote again. *You knew about the robbery ahead of time?*

"No! I... I was afraid that something was being brewed. I had no idea what it was or when it was going to happen. Not then. But if I didn't get you out of there, I was afraid something might have happened to you."

To me?

Yes, to him. "You're like a super-cop, Jay. You'll do whatever it takes for the good of everyone else. Like when you got shot a few months ago." She shook her head. "But I couldn't take a chance on the wrong people spotting me. Recognizing me." She let her gaze rest on his. "That's the truth of it."

And it was. Not her entire story, but she had a

clear conscience with all she'd said.

After a long moment, he nodded. "Cal knows this?"

"You're not supposed to talk, remember?"

He emitted a heavy sigh. How tough for him to simply lie there and let people talk around him without being able to comment or question. "Cal knows. So does Captain Madison."

She straightened a tissue box, a pitcher of water, and a glass of ice on the tray that stretched across his bed from the other side of it. "You want some water?"

He took her hand and held it in both of his. "I want you to know…."

"Aannt." Cal chose that moment to reenter. "I promised the doc that I wouldn't let you talk and I'm keeping my promise." He glanced at Dani. "You have another job. Ty's talking on the phone with someone named Frank, but he's headed in here. Said he'll take you to the scene once he gets to split a hair with Jay."

Split a hair? Sounded like Tyrone.

"Where's that lazy, good-for-nothing." Ty burst in. Dani stepped aside and let him give Jay half of a man-hug. "Can't let you outta my sight for one night? What is this? Dani, don't you have a leash or something for this guy?"

She shrugged. Ty knew less about her than Jay did and she needed to keep it that way.

With both of them.

Chapter Eleven

The moment he'd laid eyes on Dani, Jay knew his heart could settle on no one else. Despite his irritation at her secrets and half-answers, he wanted to believe in her. Even if he couldn't fully trust everything she said.

But with his near death came a conviction that he couldn't proceed without God's approval. *You know my heart, Father. You alone can change it. Please change it if you don't want Dani and me to be together.*

As hard as it would be for him to accept God's negative answer, he steeled himself to do it and prayed that the answer would be obvious enough for him to recognize it.

After Cal walked them out, he strolled in with a bag of cocoa-covered almonds. "Sorry to tease you like this, but I'm starved. Guess it's gonna be a bit before you can have something crunchy again." He popped a couple in his mouth.

Jay glared at him, but the guy only laughed. "I'll get you a chocolate malt on your way home, k?"

He helped Jay to the edge of the bed. "So we're looking for a guy named Tonio Ventinelli."

Jay stilled to let the fuzziness in his mind fade.

"He mighta been the guy who tied up the wound." Cal moved a walker into position.

Jay tapped the pad to get his partner's attention. *Not the one who stabbed him?*

"No reason to think that." Cal helped him to his feet. "You good?"

The ground swayed for a moment but settled back into a mostly horizontal foundation. As Jay stepped into the hallway, he discarded the walker and gripped Cal's arm instead. How did Tonio Ventinelli fit into the equation? Was that the name of the man who had car-jacked him? The wicked eyes peeking from under the blue hoodie flashed across his memory. He needed to describe him to Alfred Jackson, the artist who worked for the department, so he could work up a composite.

Jay paused halfway down the hall.

"You need to go back? Feeling dizzy? Doc said you might."

Jay shook his head. "Need to get to work."

"Ha. Fat chance, buddy-o." He took another step, but Jay pulled back.

"Find a way for me to get out of here." The whisper sounded garbled even to Jay's ears, but he became more determined with every step that the pieces had all been laid out, and he needed to assemble them.

Cal's jowls sagged. "Look. You coulda died. The doc still isn't sure how you got away without any major damage."

A jaw wired shut and bruises coloring half his body seemed like damage enough.

"You need to take it easy and let yourself heal for a bit. Just do what the doc says."

Jay pointed back down the hallway toward his room.

"Okay, okay. But you get there and write me out some instructions. You're going to stay here and heal." His partner grabbed his arm and kept him stabilized on the way back to his bed.

He'd obey, like Cal said, at least until lunch. His stomach gurgled. And if he was lucky, he could purloin a laptop and do a little research on Tonio Ventinelli.

"'Bout time you roused. I've sent your soup back three times to be reheated."

Cal's gruff voice pulled Jay from his fog. "Did

I fall asleep?" Ow. Oh, yeah. No talking.

"Yeah. About three hours' worth of nap-time"

Jay glanced at the clock and accepted the large Styrofoam cup his partner handed him. Two-forty? A simple walk down the hall had solidly flattened him. He sipped the warm chicken stock through the straw. Ugh. But necessary. Next time, he wanted the milkshake that should have been in this cup. Strawberry.

"Don't sweat it. Your body needs to heal." He hoisted a black and tan backpack into the chair next to him. "But I had Gutierrez bring by your laptop."

Jay popped his thumb up and reached for it.

"Yeah, I thought that would make you smile. Or at least not grimace." He extracted it from the special bag and set it up on the table spanning Jay's bed while he continued to force down the bland soup. "So... what are we looking at, first?"

Jay opened the research tab and typed in *Tonio Ventinelli*.

"I see. But are you trying to find out about him

or about Dani?"

Information about Dani hadn't crossed his mind. Was there a strong connection between the two?

He pointed at Tonio's name as the server updated.

Antonio Giraldo Ventinelli, age thirty-four and born in New York City, had a long list of credits to his name including fraud, assault, burglary, and other assorted thefts.

"This guy's a charmer." Cal tucked a toothpick into his mouth.

High school drop-out. Charm school flunkie. How had Dani even met a guy like this?

"Let's get a look at this guy." Cal pointed to the image button that showed up at the top right corner of the page.

The smiling face of a deeply tanned, muscular Italian showed up.

Jay's soup hit the pit of his stomach. Tonio Ventinelli was the waiter who had shown him out the back way and sent him for his car. The connection to Dani was obviously there. Had they… had she?

"Huh. I guess, he musta caught Dani's eye."

Jay growled his response. And if that were the case, no wonder she'd tried to protect him.

"But I think you captured her heart, kid."

Cal? A romantic? Since when? Jay arched his left eyebrow, with a twinge of pain, and stared at his partner.

"What? I got eyes. And besides, she gave up the man's name and everything she knew about him the moment she heard you were hurt." He folded his arms. "That speaks volumes, huh."

Jay glanced back at the picture. Whoever the guy was, Cal was right. Dani hadn't kept quiet about him when Jay's life was at stake. That knowledge made looking at the photo easier, but only by a little.

He flicked to another picture with Tonio alongside a pair of businessmen in rapt conversation. He pivoted the laptop screen toward Cal.

"Looks like he played bodyguard for some big fish. Recognize the men?"

Jay shook his head and clicked on a button for more details. The date and time popped up—from about eighteen months ago—along with the link to another file. He hit that button.

A new tab opened with a security bar and a request for the access code. Jay had seen pages like this before when his cases drifted into the scope of a federal investigation.

Great. He lifted his eyes to the ceiling.

"FBI from the looks of it." Cal's toothpick twitched.

"I don't like it." Jay's voice sounded raspy and his throat burned. He slurped water through a straw and tried again. "If Dani's still involved with him…."

"I know. Let's check on the other images."

Maybe he'd spot the blue-hoodie guy. He

returned to the first page and scanned down the images one at a time. Tonio had been caught with the same businessman several times in various places. He'd also had his share of girls on his arm. Parties, street views, usually in groups or with the suit patrol.

None of the photos gave identification, and the latest was from fourteen months earlier. April, last year. He pointed. "Most recent."

The picture wasn't as crisp as some of the others but showed Tonio smiling and looking to the right of the camera, as though he was talking to someone.

The same businessman from several pictures stood a dozen or so yards behind him. Slightly blurred, but definitely the same guy. He was talking with a woman. Nice legs in wedge sandals and perfectly styled platinum waves. Her back was to the camera, but she had a good figure.

He froze and pointed to the screen. The woman had stacked her weight onto her right foot with her left leg extended, and her left arm circled the back of her waist to wrap her hand around her right elbow.

That had to be Dani.

Chapter Twelve

Dani ran the carpet cleaner over the space one more time. She shut off the machine and inspected the spot before removing her gloves and mask.

"Done out here." She tugged the ponytail holder out of her hair. "How's the kitchen looking?"

"Spic and span, of course." Tyrone advanced down the hallway between the bathrooms. "Not that there was much more to do but sweep up all of the fingerprint dust."

"Did we get the blood in the pantry up?" There hadn't been much, but its presence was a health hazard.

"Done." Tasha carried her helmet in one hand and a cleaning bucket full of supplies in the other. "And I threw everything from there away, per instructions."

"Good." Tyrone tugged his gloves off and glanced at his watch. "I vote we wait for Frank at the cheesecake place across the parking lot."

He didn't have to twist Dani's arm. She brought up the rear to load the van and stole a glance down the lot where Jay had parked his car the other night. An image flitted past of him leaning against his gun-metal gray Charger. Arms and ankles crossed, as she'd seen him so many times when he came to check up on his scenes.

But only the bare lot sulked. He'd stopped his visits with his promotion. Besides, his car had been totaled.

Pity.

At least he'd been released. After two days, they'd had to let him out, or he would have found a way to escape.

"You said there was another robbery in McKinney." Tasha guided on the cart as Dani shoved it up the ramp to the back of the big white box truck that held their gear. She smoothed her cork-screw curls. Resembled the hair that Dani had in her former life, only Tasha's had the glow of a natural yellow blond instead of the bleach and perm of Dani's do.

"Two robberies? Same M.O.?" Ty shook his head. "Surely the cops have a lead?"

They did. Tonio. Though Dani had no way of knowing if the man was still involved with the ring.

"Cal told me that he's communicating with the McKinney PD. There's not much to go on." Dani climbed into the cab behind Tasha.

"And when did you speak to Cal?" Ty's eye had a knowing gleam to it.

"I helped him move Jay home yesterday."

"Ohhh. You moved Jay home." His mahogany skin made his toothy grin practically glow.

"Careful." Tasha laid a hand on his arm. "You're beginning to sound like a pre-adolescent, middle-school boy."

"Yeah, and if you don't chill, I'll tattle to your wife." Dani smirked.

Tasha let off a tremble of giggles as Ty pulled out of his two parking spaces. "So back to the robberies. Could the similarities be a fluke?"

No way. Not with the strange methods. She shook her head. "The wait staff was collected one by one and sleep-gassed while the crooks took their places." Dani paused. "Could have been a copycat, but I can't imagine two groups dreaming that up at the same time."

Ty parked in front of the stone facade building. A downright decadent aroma wafted around them. Until the thick scent of Frank Durmondo's cheap cologne strangled out the lovely scent.

"Hi, boss." Ty spread a bright smile. "Your treat?" He pointed to the sign.

"Hardly." The man grimaced above his outdated, pencil-thin soul-patch. He barely reached Ty's armpit, in both height and personality, and even in the summer, he wore a knotted scarf like some 1940's producer caricature.

All he needed was the painter's cap to complete the cartoon.

"You don't have time for a snack. One of the suburban teams called in sick."

"The entire team?" Tasha's eyebrow lifted as her golden head bobbed to one side.

"They all went out for barbecue after their shift last night. They think it was the macaroni salad."

Ugh. Suddenly cheesecake didn't sound so very yummy. "And we need to fill in for them."

"Yes, and you were due two hours ago." Frank turned Dani back toward the truck and urged her forward. "The restaurant is all the way in McKinney, so you need to get a move on." He gave Tasha a little push toward the passenger door.

Tyrone put his hands on his hips, daring the man to shove him. "Is this place the new robbery we've heard about. Like the one here at Bella Noda?"

"Don't know. Don't care." Frank brushed his fingers several times like he was trying to herd Tyrone into the truck. "But time is money. Get the truck in gear and head north."

Ty turned slowly toward Dani. A glare showed his eyes. "Next time, use the phone to call us ahead of time." He turned back to face Frank, halting the smaller man from hurrying behind him. "You do know how to do that, don't you?"

Frank's mouth tightened into an o. He slipped his phone from his pocket, but at least he didn't follow Ty all the way to the truck.

Climbing in, Ty let the odd glare fall off his face and replaced it with his traditional grin. "I'll bet his phone is smarter than he is."

Tasha giggled.

Dani glanced out at Frank who was texting something. His thumbs bouncing furiously over his keyboard. He looked up and caught her eye. His face turned stony, casting pure hate in their direction.

Or was his look focused on her alone?

Sleeping in his own bed had finally taken the edge off of some of Jay's soreness, until his morning appointment with his physical therapist. And with Cal as his chauffeur, he couldn't very well let on how much every movement hurt.

He groaned, popped a pain killer, and took a swig from the straw stuck into his water bottle. At least he could open his mouth. If only he could do it without the excruciating pain. He tucked the bottle into the cup holder on the console between his seat and Cal's.

"A shame your therapist is such a bully." Cal smirked. "Otherwise, she was a knockout."

"I gotta girl." Jay's voice cracked, and he slurped again from the straw as Cal exited the freeway. "Restaurant's over there." He pointed to a line of upscale restaurants, and Cal slowed the car. "Tyndalhaus. Behind the Tex Mex place."

Cal turned his brown Chevy Cavalier left down a main artery. "A German restaurant? I don't connect German food with expensive, uber high-society places."

Jay lightly massaged both sides of his jaw. "Artistic" He pointed to the sign beneath the eatery's name that labeled it *Eclectic Cuisine.*

"I remember now. It's supposed to have some famous chef from one of those shows on a foodie network."

Jay nodded. As they pulled into the front of the place, he recognized a detective from his department. Durwood. It wasn't so unusual for one of them to want to discuss a case with Jay now that he was a team lead, but calling him in for a debriefing with another town's department was a little out of the ordinary. "Why are we here?"

"What do you mean 'we'? You're the only

towel hanging on this line. You were first man on the scene. And your girlfriend has connections to the thieves. One of them at least." Cal shoved the car into park and turned toward him. "Did you ask her about that picture you found?"

How could he? He shook his head, though his gut told him it had to be her, even with the weird hair.

Durwood was talking with two men in ties and dress coats. They looked about as uncomfortable as Jay felt. Another big guy had his back to them. He wore canvas shorts and a yellow tee shirt.

Jay got out and started in that direction.

"Is that your friend?" Cal joined him.

From the back, it sure looked like Tyrone, but what would he be doing up here?

"The site hasn't been released, yet. Give us another hour." One of the guys Jay didn't know was looking up at the Tyrone look-alike.

Jay neared and confirmed the identification of his friend. "Ty." He shook the man's hand.

"Surprised to see you, but I'm glad you're vertical." His friend gave him a quick pat on the back, thankfully not the pounding he usually got.

Tasha rounded the corner. The movement caught Jay's attention. Dani followed. His chest convulsed slightly at the sight of her. Not that she hadn't been around, but the meds he'd been on were such that he barely remembered his own name. If only his mind had been fully functioning. Maybe they could have had more of a meaningful conversation than what he wanted to eat for dinner. Not that it had mattered, since he'd fallen asleep as soon as he'd made it home.

She stopped short when her eyes locked with his, then her chin drifted down and she continued in his direction.

Ty shook hands with Cal. "He giving you much trouble?"

"Always." Cal smirked. "Aren't you a little out of your zone?"

"Indeed. But orders are orders." He nodded to

the two McKinney men. "Only I've been told we can't clean up, yet. Meanwhile, the restaurant wants to reopen tonight."

"An hour at the most." The two men led Durwood toward the front door.

Jay glanced at his phone. Already after noon. They'd be hard-pressed to get things clean enough for dinner tonight. "Sorry, man." He clapped his hand against Ty's shoulder.

Dani stepped closer and peered into his face. Her dark eyes pierced into thoughts and emotions he'd been trying to shut away. "You... okay?"

His hand lifted—longing to touch her shoulder, her cheek, but he let it fall back to his side. "I will be."

She gave a flat-lipped smile.

"Maybe...." He blew out a breath. He needed to speak to her. Needed her to speak to him. But would she shut him down?

She tilted her head and lifted her shoulders a bit.

"Can we talk?" There. It was up to her, now.

Her lashes lowered along with her shoulders. Like she was bracing herself against a strong wind.

"You coming?" Durwood held the door open for him.

"Yeah." He stepped toward the entrance. "You'll be here?"

She nodded.

Good. Even if he didn't get any answers from her, maybe they could find a way for this, whatever it was that they had, to get back on the right track.

Chapter Thirteen

Even after the McKinney detectives released the site, Jay and Cal remained talking with them. Dani tried not to notice them, but Jay always had a way of drawing her attention even when he wasn't trying.

And he had her attention, now. He was pointing with a pen to the open file spread out on one of the dining room tables. First, one of the other men said something and then Jay responded. Though he kept his mouth rather still as he spoke.

His jaw must've still been hurting.

She refocused on the door frame she'd been

wiping down. Tears that she'd squashed for days blurred her eyes. He might have been killed in that wreck. Jay wouldn't show her the picture of his car, but Cal had, though not intentionally. The image had been up on his computer screen when Dani visited the hospital the day after the accident.

The whole side of the car had been crushed. The only saving grace being that the truck had hit off-center, more toward the back seat than the front, or Jay's long legs would have been pinned.

Trapped and crushed. A new tear trickled down. *Thank you, God, for taking care of him.* How could she have lived with herself? The guilt was already tearing her up. If she'd been open about Tonio from the beginning, would that have made any difference?

If she told Jay everything now, would he still care about her?

Too many ifs. She squeezed her eyes shut for a moment—blocked the guilt, released the fear. None of that would change what had happened to Jay.

And giving in to her emotions threatened the work she had to finish. Both her cleaning job and the future statements she had to make in the face of pure evil.

"You done in here?" Ty came in through the kitchen and examined one of the tables near her. "You missed a spot." He wiped down the rectangular tables and the booth seats surrounding it. "That's not like you, Dani."

She slipped her gloves off. At least they hadn't been in full hazardous gear for this job. "I've been a little distracted."

He peered into her face for a moment. She dropped her gaze and looked away.

"He's all right."

"No thanks to me." Dani sniffed. Ty knew very little of the situation, and she could explain nothing.

"I don't know about that. He sure seems to brighten when you're around."

That was doubtful. She laid her gloves in her tool bucket.

Ty tapped the table. "See there? Proves my point."

"What?" She glanced at him, but he nodded in Jay's direction. She looked toward the table of men in time to catch Jay's eyes on her. He smiled.

"Told you." He picked up Dani's tool bucket as the men stood and shook hands. "I'll take care of this. You go... talk or something."

Something. She wanted to curl her arms around his neck and feel his warm breath on her face. But that might never happen again.

She needed to choose her timing though. If he was still talking, it would be awkward for her to stand around nearby. She turned toward the entrance where they had been sitting and found Jay strolling toward her with Cal behind him.

"Hi."

The one word made her want to melt. "You look so much better."

"Standing anyway." His low voice was soft, and his jaw was stiff.

"Does it still hurt?" She winced at the sight of the stitches along the side of his jaw. When she'd seen him before, they were covered with a bandage. The view of them sewn into his skin made her stomach topple.

He nodded. "Glad I can talk, though. Hard to chew."

"Good thing there's soup."

He pointed at his mouth and stuck his tongue out.

From watching him the past few days, if survival meant living on broth, he was doomed. "Smoothies?" She'd brought him a milkshake the day before. Especially in this heat, something like that should go over well.

He gave a lopsided smile, probably due to his stiffness, but his left jaw might've still been a little swollen.

Cal reached them and completed the triangle. "I'm going back with Durwood. Got another idea I want to send past him."

"Your car?" Jay raised his eyebrows.

"That's why I'm giving the keys to her." Cal held them out to Dani. "Make the man eat something before you take him back to the department." He eyed Jay. "I trust you can figure out a way to get her home?"

A tiny smile widened the right side of Jay's face as he nodded. Cal strode away, and Jay turned his eyes onto her. "Do you mind?" He held out his hand.

She didn't deserve his kindness. Squeezing away her fears, she met his gaze and shook her head, placing her hand in his.

His closeness and warmth pervaded her body. But could his affection last when the questions began?

Jay switched the air conditioning fan to high and leaned his aching head against the rest. "You don't have to do this. I can drive myself back."

"Yes, I do. There goes my ride." Dani pointed at the white box truck as it turned left out of the parking lot. *Kellerman's Crisis and Trauma Cleaning* marched horizontally along its side.

She glanced at him. "But I don't mind. You have to believe that."

After her many visits to the hospital and her taking time off to help Cal get him settled at home, she'd proved that she cared.

Still, she hadn't shared much from the night of the robbery.

"Have you heard anything from your friend? Tonio, right?" He gave her a sidelong look.

She kept her eyes steady on the road. "Cal tell you about that?"

"Was it secret?"

Without answering, she merged onto the Dallas North Tollway. "I haven't heard from him. And I don't expect to. Ever."

"You happened to see him?" This wasn't

exactly where he wanted to take their conversation, but the elephant was practically squeezing the air out of the car.

"You don't still think that I had something to do with that robbery." Her eyes widened as she took an exit.

He shook his head. "No, sweetheart. I knew you were hiding something. That's all." He lowered his head. "You still are. I wish you could trust me."

She slowed, turned in to the parking lot of a Tom Thumb, and stopped under a tree. She stared at the steering wheel for a moment, tracing her finger around its circumference, and exhaled heavily before looking at him. "It's not about trust, Jay. It's about… there are things in my past that… can't come out." She went back to staring at her fingers resting on the leather covered circle. "I'm not that person anymore."

"I care about the woman you are now. Not about anything that's happened before." He leaned forward and stroked her cheek.

"I believe you." She locked her gaze with his. "I trust you with my life, Jay. I always have." She took his hand in both of hers. "But you have to trust me, too. Even through my secrets."

His gaze lowered. She still wouldn't open up.

"I hope you can do that." She dipped her head.

"I'll try." He touched her chin. "You're certainly worth it to me."

She didn't exactly smile, but her face relaxed. She put the car back into gear and pulled out into the street. "So will Fro-Yo work for you, or Smoothie Shack?"

"Smoothie sounds good." Especially in the sweltering heat. "Have you thought anymore about going home with me over the Fourth?" Maybe he shouldn't have jumped from one uncomfortable topic to another, but at least they could push them both out of the way.

"You still want me to?" A little pucker formed between her brows.

"Of course." As much as before. Maybe even

more.

She cut her eyes in his direction. "I'm still thinking about it. When do you have to know?"

"My mom is hoping you'll come. Keeps after me to convince you."

Dani parked in an open spot at the storefront of a smoothie shop.

He climbed out and met her at the front of the car, slipping his hand around her waist. "She's gonna love you." He pulled her closer and planted a light kiss against her hair. The light fragrance of honeysuckle somewhat eased his pain from the movement.

The wrinkle deepened between her brows. "Do you really think so or are you only trying to make me feel more at ease?"

He cupped her cheek. "She and I are exactly alike." He drifted closer. "And I think you're amazing." His lips found hers, but even the slight touch riveted pain through his head. He pulled back.

She pinked and touched his right jaw. "Oh, I'm so sorry."

Not as much as he was, and not from the pain of her kiss. More from the absence of it.

But her kisses would have to wait. Right along with the answers he still hoped for.

Dani toyed with her straw and glanced up at Jay. He was watching her across the table.

"What?"

"You have an overbite." The semblance of a grin spread slightly before he winced.

"Anything else you want to criticize?" She pursed her lips together.

"No, not criticize. I think it's cute." He took another slurp from his straw.

The edges of her mouth pulled against her clamped lips.

Before she could come up with a clever

response, his phone played the theme from some old police show. Uh, oh.

"Hunter." He held the phone to his right ear and looked away from her. "Yeah, she's right here."

Someone was asking about her? Why? Had they found Tonio? Or did someone else know where she was?

He stood, but let his gaze drift down to her. "Yeah. We'll be right there." He slipped the phone into his pocket.

"*We'll?* As in you and me?" She stayed in her seat but looked up at him.

"The captain is calling us to the scene of another robbery." He took another drink from his cup and tossed it in the trashcan.

"Again, who is us? Us as in your crime scene investigation team, or us as in us-us?"

He put his hand on the back of her chair as she scooted it out. "You and me. Particularly you." He moved to the door and held it open for her. "But the bigger question would be why is Madison there?"

She paused when she got to the front of the car. "Is that such a strange thing?"

"He rarely goes to scenes. Maybe three scenes since I started working them. Going on seven years." Jay held the passenger door for her.

Something was up. Something big. "Wait. What about me?" Had Madison said something to Jay about her past? Or maybe Matthew had changed his mind about leaving her in Dallas. That would get the captain involved, but not at a crime scene.

Jay shut the door on her question and rounded the car to the driver's side before answering. "I don't know. He said something about Tonio Ventinelli."

At another robbery? She shut her eyes. Why had he gotten back involved with that group? "Has he been arrested?" That would be the best for him, but the man knew far too much for her good.

After shoving the seat backward, Jay adjusted

the mirrors. "Not sure."

"I thought I was supposed to be driving."

"That was Cal's way of getting you and me together." He started the engine and shifted gears. "I'm fine."

"So about Tonio...." She had to know. Had to find some way to divert Jay.

"You know as much as I do, honey. The captain asked me to bring you to another restaurant. Apparently, another robbery, though he didn't say as much."

Oh, no. Why had Tonio kept it up? Especially after the guy he was working for actually stabbed him? She looked out the window at the silent world speeding past.

Jay seemed to have nothing to say, but his face still held a slight smile when he looked at her. That wouldn't happen once Tonio opened his mouth.

Oh, God, I don't deserve any protection from my mistakes in the past, but please don't let Tonio give me away.

Chapter Fourteen

Jay let the quiet deepen. The captain's reluctance to explain the situation placed a heavy weight on his shoulders. But without any explanation, he didn't dare divulge his own fears.

The fact that Tonio was on site had to mean he'd been apprehended. Dani must've surmised that much. Maybe through the interrogation, Jay would learn some of the answers he longed for.

Hopefully Dani wouldn't hate him for wanting to know.

He stole a glimpse of her. The wrinkle on her forehead had returned. How he wanted to permanently remove that worry line from her face. His embraces and encouragement could only do so much. There were things she'd have to work through on her own.

If only she'd let him help her.

He steered the car toward a brick, stand-alone restaurant, set away from the road and rather secluded with a creek on one side. Trudiano's Eatery. This one didn't seem as high class as the others. Why it popped up on the radar of this ring of thieves he couldn't tell.

"Odd place for a robbery." Dani tensed and leaned forward. "Why would the crooks come here?"

Jay shook his head. "No clue. Third one. Every other day, if they are connected like they seem to be."

"There has to be some reason behind their choices." She didn't allow him time to open her door for her, but he met her in front of the car.

She put her hand on his chest. "The captain

wanted me, right?"

"He said something about Tonio."

"Then let me go in. I can talk to Tonio. Get him to listen to reason. He'll tell the captain what he knows." She turned away from Jay and trotted up the steps.

She didn't want him in there. He sighed. More secrets. He took a half-step backward.

No. His job was in there. And so was the woman he... whatever. He wasn't about to be dismissed by misplaced fear and unnecessary deception. He jogged toward the entrance.

His eyes had to adjust to the dim interior. Several people, wait staff and likely customers, sat in the dining room where a few officers moved from table to table taking statements. Jay caught the flash of a dark pony tail disappearing into the kitchen and followed.

"No." Dani's raised voice propelled him through the door.

She spun, and he caught her in his arms as she

burst into tears.

He embraced her and peered over her shoulder where a white-sheeted figure lay against the far wall. He glared at Captain Madison. "You couldn't have warned her?"

"With her way of life, I couldn't have been sure I was getting the straight story without allowing a small shock."

"Forcing her to find the body of a friend isn't a small shock, Captain." His word came out as a growl between clenched teeth and an aching jaw.

"Settle down, kid." Cal stepped closer and laid a meaty palm on his shoulder. "She'll be all right."

Dani sniffed. "I'm fine." She pushed back from Jay and whirled on the captain. "Tonio was messed up with his ideas of how to survive and who to trust. But he was a good person. A kind person. Not like you."

The captain's eyebrow twitched. "If I've erred, I'm sorry."

"*If* you've erred. Translation: 'I'll say I'm

sorry, but I don't really mean it.'" She turned and buried her face against Jay's chest. His eyes narrowed as he stared at his boss.

"Let me try again, then." He stepped toward them both. "It is apparent that I have erred in my strategy to learn the truth about these robberies. I'm very sorry that my actions hurt you. My intention was to find an honest response, not to hurt you."

When Dani didn't move, he glanced up to Jay and held his gaze for a moment. Seemed the man was sincere, though Jay wanted to tell him off. Instead, he looked down and pulled back to catch Dani's eyes. "I'm sorry, honey. Sorry about Tonio most of all. And sorry that you're hurting."

She squeezed her eyes shut for a moment, then released the grip she had on his shirt front. Her sad look was somehow mixed with guilt, but he only saw it for a moment before she again faced the captain. "I've told you all I can about Tonio. You know everything that I know."

"Probably more." Madison turned and

collected a book from one of the other officers. He held it up. "Recognize this?"

Was that Dani's...?

"My Bible? Where did you get it?" She reached for it, but he pulled it back.

"Maybe I should tell you that before we found him here, we had located a motel room where he'd been staying." Madison gave her a stern look. Almost like a disappointed father.

Dani turned her head slightly and waited for a moment. "Is that supposed to mean something to me?"

"We found this there. In his room. Strange thing to take with you to such a place."

"Oh, come on, Captain." Jay took a step forward.

Cal pulled him back with both arms wrapped around his chest. "Easy, there." He lowered his voice to a whisper. "You know your girl can deliver as good as you, and she can't get fired for it."

Jay expelled a breath, but the pressure inside

didn't release. The heat from outside seemed to fill the interior of the kitchen.

Dani's shoulders straightened. "You should get your mind out of the gutter more often, Captain." She practically spat out his rank. "The filthy mold is starting to take root."

"You weren't at Tonio's hotel room." Madison's chin jutted toward her.

"No." She straightened. Cal was right about her. "Don't ask again."

"Very well." He retreated somewhat and laid the Bible on the counter. "How did such a man come to have a Bible, with your name on the inside cover, in his hotel room?"

"Now that is the question you should have asked the first time. Instead of making insulting assumptions… for which you have not apologized." She crossed her arms.

"Apologize for what?" The captain's armor showed a chink as exasperation filled his tone.

"For publicly insinuating erroneous flaws on

my character that could permanently damage my reputation. Have you been so long around corruption and people with no morality that you can't see someone who *does* have strong values?"

Jay wanted to applaud.

The man positively growled. "Strong values? Really?" His eyes twinkled. "With all the things I know about you, Miss Foster, I'm somewhat amused by your little rant."

"Now just a minute." Jay pushed against Cal's arms.

"Calm down." Cal turned toward Madison. "It wouldn't do to make all three of us mad, Captain."

The man held up both palms. "Fine. It seems, Miss Foster, that I have once again offended. Forgive me. Could you please tell me how Tonio Ventinelli came into possession of your Bible?"

She glanced back at Jay. The guilty expression had returned. "I told you that he was injured after the Bella Noda robbery."

"Yes, he'd come up to you at the bus stop.

Then on that bus, he explained what had happened." The captain had added a sing-song tone to his voice.

"All that is true. Everything he told me." Dani's gaze darted from one face to another. "But I didn't tell you that he pretended to hold a knife on me."

Jay flinched. She considered this man a friend? "He assaulted you?"

"No. He was simply desperate. He needed a place to hide and rest." She lowered her gaze to his toes. "I took him to my apartment."

Ruidosa, who had been standing near the back door, started scribbling on his notepad.

"He needed medical attention. I told him that, but he was afraid the doctors' questions would get him police attention that he didn't want."

"Didn't you realize how dangerous that was?" Jay couldn't coax her to look at him.

"I knew what Tonio was capable of, but for some reason, I wasn't afraid of him."

She'd known him and his suited friends. Jay had been right about that picture he'd found.

The captain stepped forward, like he wanted the spotlight back. "And the Bible?"

"His injury got him to thinking about eternal matters. I tried to speak with him about God, and he seemed to listen. So I handed him my Bible and showed him some verses that might help him find truth and comfort." She met Jay's gaze for an instant. "Romans." She turned back to the captain. "I noticed it was gone when I realized that he'd left."

"So he took it with him when he left? When was that?"

"I can't be sure. He was gone when Cal brought me back to my apartment."

Cal startled at that tidbit. "You mean that guy was there when I came to get you?" His gaze hit the ceiling. "I shoulda known by the way you were dressed and your nervous glances toward your bedroom. I just thought you were uncomfortable because I was at your apartment."

"I'm sorry." Her chin dropped. "I couldn't tell you. I thought I was helping."

"About got your man there killed."

"Cal." Jay stepped between them and wrapped an arm around Dani. "Taking care of a friend isn't ever wrong. But you can always tell me."

The captain cleared his throat, turned the book page-down and gave it a shake. Nothing came out, but he flipped the pages a few times to be sure. "I suppose I can return this to you." He held out the book.

She took it and embraced it, her eyes beginning to redden again. "I don't know what other answers I have."

"Do I need to make a call to your… friend?"

"No." The finality of her tone held an icy edge.

The captain looked at her for a long minute. "This is messy business. Getting worse by the day."

Time to give Dani a chance to breathe and collect herself. Jay pointed toward the white sheet covering the body. "So how did this happen?"

"Your guess is as good as mine. I mean, we know he was shot. We also know that the rest of the thieves got away without completing the robbery." He wiped sweat from his forehead.

"Quick call and response?"

He shook his head. "Nothing like that. They were gone when we got here." He pointed to a refrigerator door. "Another body in there, apparently the owner of this place. He was stabbed on location. But Ventinelli…."

Jay wandered closer to the sheet while the captain spoke. He knelt and pulled it back slightly to shield Dani from the view. The man underneath had been dead for some time. Beaten severely before he was shot. And the only blood that showed was a small stain on his shirt. Jay lowered his voice almost to a whisper. "He was dumped here."

Chapter Fifteen

Thankfully, the captain didn't mention calling Matthew again. He gave Dani permission to leave. She turned to the door with Jay's hand at her back.

"I still need you here, Hunter." Madison was quickly becoming her least favorite person, even surpassing both Matthew and Frank.

"I'll be back, then. Especially with all that's gone on, I'm not letting Dani out of my sight until she's safely back home." His fingers drifted down to entwine with hers.

The man paused, obviously processing his response. "All right. Cal here will brief you when you get back to the station."

Jay guided her out of the kitchen and through the dining room where customers still spoke to police. "That bought us a little time alone."

A week ago, that thought would have thrilled her. But at this point, she couldn't shake her fear of having to tell Jay how she knew Tonio. Not to mention all of the others he ran with and how she fit in.

In silence, she took her seat in Cal's dingy sedan. Surely Jay wouldn't press. Not after all she'd been through.

Before he started the engine, he stroked her cheek. "I really am sorry about what happened in there, honey, but it's going to be okay."

She let the tension ease out of her with his touch. "I hope you're right." If only she could hold the moment. But the best she could do was catch his hand and plant a light kiss on his knuckle. "Thanks for taking up for me in there."

"I meant what I said. You don't have to be

afraid."

She strapped her seatbelt on and hoped he wouldn't start interrogating her. Even though she deserved his questions.

He remained quiet, though. For most of the trip she watched the lights of Dallas outside her window and thought about poor Tonio. Had he found any peace with God? Had Dani done all she could to tell him about Jesus?

Where she expected guilt, a glimmer of hope grew. Dani hadn't been any more in charge of that conversation than Tonio had orchestrated their chance meeting. God had a purpose in it. Surely, He saw it through to the best possible end.

She turned and studied the man who as often as not inhabited her dreams. Lights danced across his profile, but she knew his face as well as she knew her own. A five o'clock shadow barely grazed his strong jawline and threaded along his upper lip. His straight nose gave a hint at his ancestry as much as his tanned skin did.

He cut his eyes toward her. "Feeling a little better?"

She nodded and reached for his hand that rested on his centered gear-shift. "I think, I'm not sure, but I'm hopeful that Tonio accepted Christ as his Savior. The passage he'd been reading…." She opened the book to Romans. This was a powerful section that laid out the need for a Savior and the inability for people to save themselves no matter how good they tried to be. "I think he…." Her fingers drifted over a new note written in the margin underneath one of her own.

You were right about everything, Sammi. If only I'd listened to you before.

Well, before she'd not been so very focused on the Lord. Had she even shown His love or grace?

The sharp manuscript ran off the bottom of the page and Dani turned it. *Glad God sent you back to me. The bag is in your court now.*

Bag? She squinted. Plainly the word he wrote was bag. Maybe he'd only meant to say ball.

Especially in October when it gets colder.

October. If she could make it until then. Not that it gets so very cold in Dallas at that point, but then Tonio wouldn't have reason to know that. But he did know that the end of her journey, and possibly a new beginning, came in October.

"You thought he what?" Jay toyed with the knob of gear shift.

"Oh, just that I think he took the Scriptures to heart." She hoped he had. Another set of tears stung the back of her eyes, and she blinked. She had to stop crying. Tonio was in a tough business, and he was no child. He'd given as often as he'd received, and probably as violently, though she didn't like thinking about that.

"Was he a good friend?"

Such a simple question, but there was no easy answer for it. The man hadn't been good in any form of the word. And he hadn't really been a friend, although he'd helped her when it counted. That meant something, right? "He was there when

I needed him. Got us out of the restaurant. I'd say that was a good friend." Sort of.

"But you'd known him before."

"I don't have anything to add to what you've already heard." And the last thing she needed was Sergeant Hunter conducting a private interrogation.

"Whoa, whoa. I'm not interested in his illegalities… well, at least that's not the purpose… I mean, I'm more interested in your—that is, yours and his—relationship. The guy put his life in jeopardy to make you safe. He must've cared for you quite a lot." Jay glanced at her before turning his attention back to the road.

Wow. Jay was right. Tonio had cared. He must have.

The tires began to whine as the asphalt gave way to grooved concrete. The smaller, worn interior of Cal's car made her impression of Jay's destroyed Charger grow exponentially.

Jay kept his eyes on the road. He deserved an answer.

"You might be right, but I can't really speak to his feelings. There was nothing but air between us, though I appreciated his help and wanted him to find peace with an understanding of God's grace." Hopefully, Jay would read nothing more into that than the truth.

He nodded. "You have a beautiful heart, Dani."

Sighing, she drew her feet onto the seat. Something she would never have done in the pristine leather seats of Jay's cruiser, but this Cavalier's cloth seat had crumbs and stains. Her tennis shoes weren't going to make a problem.

Pushing the gearshift into park outside her building, he unlatched his safety belt and turned in his seat. "I don't know why the Lord has sent you into my life, but I'm grateful to Him."

He stroked her cheek and tucked an escaped strand of hair behind her ear. His soft touch left a warm trail across her cheek. "You're very special to me." She held her breath. Could she tell him more? Confess her internal conflict or the depth of that benign word, special?

His hand lowered to the console between them, and he looked down. "I know there are things you can't tell me. I'm an investigator, so that's pretty hard to accept. But I'm willing to."

"Willing?" What was he saying?

He stroked her hand and lifted it to his lips. "You're worth it, Dani. If you don't feel you can tell me, I've decided that no longer matters." He leaned closer and slipped his arm around her shoulders. "Nothing matters as long as…" His eyes searched her face. "…as long as I can have you by my side."

She reached for his kiss, placing her hands on each side of his face, though gently across his stitches. His arm tightened around her as his angle changed and the kiss deepened. Oh, if only she could stay in the moment. This moment. Nothing and no one… except Jay. Only his warmth surrounding her and his body close to her. To have such a man actually love her.

Her. With her rebellion and bitterness. Her history and failings. Her associates and greed. The greed that had flung her into such filth and blinded her from seeing the truth of her desperate situation. No. She didn't deserve and could never accept such a man.

Pushing back against his chest, she gasped for a breath and reached for her door latch. "I should go in."

A haunted expression of regret and shame colored Jay's face as he climbed from his side of the car and jogged around it to meet her. "I've upset you."

"No. I'm fine." Flaming hot after such a passionate kiss, but fine nonetheless. It wasn't like she hadn't been kissed before. Only, not by a man she'd grown so attached to. And for the right reasons, the virtuous ones like his honor and the way he respected people he encountered. His honesty. Oh, boy, did she love that about him. And when he learned that lying had become second nature to her, he'd turn away. He had every right to and should. "I'm sure Tasha's waiting for me by now."

Sounded plausible. How could she express the truth? That he was so perfect. His honor and respect and heroic courage made her the grunge between a turtle's toes.

"I'll call you tomorrow?"

"Yes. Sure. Tomorrow." That would give her a chance to get her head together and figure out how to break things off with him before she surrendered to another of his embraces.

Jay strained against the knot of sheets that had captured his ankles. Still dark outside, it was too late at five-forty-five for him to attempt sleep again.

If that's what the last six hours could be called. More like an interactive nightmare with his pillow and sheets alternating as shields and weapons. He'd battled frozen zombies, a giant octopus that turned into chains dragging him to the depths of the lake where he and his father used to fish. Then, he escaped only to find himself in mid-battle at the Alamo. No getting out of that one. He fell off the roof of the chapel, but it turned into the Tower of the Americas.

He struggled to untangle himself, puffing and covered in sweat that his apartment air conditioner couldn't address.

Why on earth did he feel so trapped? Boy, Cal would have a party psycho-analyzing his night. Especially the fact that he actually remembered so many of his dreams. Strange.

He stumbled to the bathroom and twisted the shower faucet on. His partner would likely conclude that Jay was afraid of the commitment he wanted to make to Dani.

But Jay had no problem with commitment. That was Calvin Cutter's area of expertise. The man had been with a new girl every month the first year after his divorce. Sort of a private calendar of faces and names Jay could barely keep straight.

All the while, he'd accused Jay of retreating, time and again, when things started getting serious with the girls he'd go out with. Not that there were so many, but he'd not felt forever feelings for any of them.

That's the part Cal didn't get, though. He couldn't understand Jay's desire for a forever instead of a bed-warmer.

No, the commitment wasn't the issue. Her response is what had him trapped. At this point, she'd likely run the other direction. She'd practically done that last night.

And that kiss had been a stupid move. What had he been thinking? There she was, finally beginning to trust him, and he lets loose with high-school hormones.

Stupid. Stupid. Stupid.

With each accusation, he slapped his wash

cloth against his face. The stitches along his cheek stung. Had he been allowed to get those wet? Oh, well. Too late now.

As he stepped from the shower, his phone began to play a theme song from Adam-12, a show he'd watched in reruns as a kid. That was Cal's ringtone. What was his partner doing up this early? He grabbed a towel and darted for the table beside his bed. "Hunter."

"Did I awaken Sleeping Beauty?" With that tone of voice, Jay didn't have to see Cal's smirk to know it was there.

"Wide awake already. What've you got?" How the tables had turned. Use-to-be, it was Jay who charged the station before dawn and had a handful of discovered details to share by the time Cal arrived on the scene.

"A cruiser made a traffic stop. Thought you might be interested."

"In a speeder? Why?"

"Huh-uh. Red-light runner. Seemed it was a

Mack truck with a smashed grill covered in paint chips of gun-metal gray."

His car. The truck that hit his car. "You coming?"

"Halfway there, already. And you need to arrange for a rental. I'm not chaperoning your dates. Got that?"

After last night, that might no longer be an issue. "Meet you outside."

Chapter Sixteen

Like an annoying mosquito, the beeping from across the apartment accosted Dani's ears as soon as she shut off her hair dryer. *Wake up already.* Tasha was probably in the shower and didn't hear the mind-numbing tone.

Dragging her flip-flops across the carpet made a light shushing sound to compliment the high-pitched percussion. All she needed was a tambourine to complete the ensemble. She shoved Tasha's door open and fell upon the timer—her roommate's iPad.

Blessed silence.

Wait. Where was the sound of the water from the shower? Dani poked her head through the doorway. Her vantage point showed the bathroom open and dark. Where was that girl?

She scanned the room. In addition to the iPad, which Tasha rarely was without, her backpack leaned against one leg of her bedside table. A textbook lay on the floor and another on the desk, open and with multi-colored flags adorning one edge. How did she study in the midst of such clutter?

Where could she have possibly gone without her school supplies? Wasn't she supposed to be taking a test.... Dani glanced at the iPad again. Right now? Supposed to be the last one for this summer session. Strange that Tasha left her bag and tablet behind. Had she even come home last night? Dani had fallen asleep on the couch waiting for her. Maybe something had happened....

Breathe. She was doing it again. Seeing Dracula in every shadow. Likely, Tasha was on a run. Dani must've misunderstood when she had her test.

She shuffled into the kitchen and popped open a can of Diet Pepsi. Summer simply wasn't the time to drink hot tea. Not here, even at the earliest, coolest hour. Though Jay drank coffee even in the heat of the day sometimes. How did he do that? The clock on the microwave declared he'd be at his office by now.

A shadow fell over her mind's eye. She'd only gotten a glimpse of the disappointment on his face last night. And she hadn't looked back or waved when she'd made it to her door. That was lousy of her. He had every reason to be ticked, but not as much as he was going to be when she rejected his invitation to spend the weekend with his family in Marseille.

Did she really have the strength to look into that man's captivating eyes and tell him no, to the trip and any other date he tried to set up? Maybe she should text him. With resolve, she marched back into her bedroom and picked up her phone.

Oops. Her dead phone. How had that happened? She never failed to charge it each night. She must've been more distracted by Jay's kisses than she'd thought.

Or she could stop lying to herself and admit that the man had crawled right into her heart. Whether she ended their relationship—like she should—or not, she'd never be the same after knowing him. And she'd never be able to stay in Dallas without his being a part of her life.

Wow. That revelation could spoil Matthew's plans. Maybe she shouldn't text Jay after all.

She pressed her power doohickey into the outlet and turned her phone back on. Jay had been pretty bothered last night. Warmth spread through her body at the memory of their embrace. He hadn't said he loved her, but... *as long as I can have you by my side.* That sure sounded like some strong feelings. Forever-type feelings. Not a proposal, but...

She laid the phone on the table.

Not a proposal! Maybe that was what had bothered him, the fact that he might've sounded like he was proposing when that wasn't his intention at all.

De-ding. De-ding. De-ding. Boy, someone had been trying to reach her. Dani turned the phone toward her and swiped the screen as the little alerts sounded in rapid succession. Who had called her so many times?

Tasha?

She ignored the messages that showed on her screen and hit the return call button. After a couple of rings, the line clicked open.

Dani didn't wait for a greeting. "Hey. How did you do on your test? You must've studied all night."

"So nice to finally speak to you again, Sammi." The male voice shocked her.

She froze for a moment before breathing again. "I don't know who you're talking about." Who was this and how had he gotten hold of Tasha? And how did he know Dani's name?

"Don't play with me, girl. I saw you at the restaurant. You left with Tonio." He tsked. "Such a sad state of affairs when a man turns his back on his associates for religion."

A fire ignited in her belly. "You killed Tonio."

The man's low chuckle slapped her back into reality. "I guess you clearly understand the situation, then."

He'd already murdered once, and now he was in control of Tasha. "What do you want?"

"Now, that's a question I can deal with. It always helps when folks ask that, you know?" A faint accent, maybe Northeastern or even European, colored his words. "I want your address. Simple, huh?"

He wanted to come to the apartment? How had he gotten hold of Tasha if he hadn't come here? "Why?"

"You're not in a position to argue or ask

questions, girl." A growl punctuated his sentence. "I want your address, or you'll find yourself minus one friend."

"You're a killer. How do I know you won't murder Tasha the minute I give you my address, or maybe she's already dead?" She gasped. Surely not, but he'd hurt her, if he hadn't already, if she didn't give him what he wanted.

"You don't. We've been hours trying to call you. You've been such a disappointment, Sammi."

"My name...." Wait, Tasha had her listed as *Roomie* on her phone. He didn't know her current name. Tonio must've told him her old one, but he couldn't use that to find her.

"I'm tired of waiting." His declaration was followed by a female outcry somewhere away from the phone.

"Stop it." She had to get Tasha away from the man. "Look, you have my number. Let her go. Let her call to tell me she's safe, and then I'll give you my address."

"And I'll simply believe you." He laughed.

"You know her name. With a little time, you can learn our address on your own. But I'm thinking you don't have a little time. Right?"

Silence. That might be a good thing. After a moment, he continued, "Agreed." The phone clicked dead.

Agreed? Would he actually release Tasha? And if so, then what did he want with Dani?

This joker wasn't worth Jay's time.

Shin Hammond sat on the narrow curb outside the trucking firm where they'd found him. Cocky, even with his hands cuffed behind his back, he leaned against the brick wall of the building and grinned up at Jay under a bushy uni-brow. "Surprised to see you standing, Officer." Funny how the title sounded like a dirty word.

Jay crossed his arms. "Your boss's name?"

"Puddin-tane." He chuckled until Cal squatted and put a fist against his throat.

"You don't get it, jerk. You tried to kill a cop—my partner."

"Easy, Sergeant." Lieutenant Gates laid a hand on Cal's shoulder. "Why don't you make sure the boys get all of the paint chips off of that grill."

Cal eased away as Jay's superior helped the suspect to his feet. "This man answering your questions, Hunter?"

"Not so much."

"What's the matter, sonny?" Gates took hold of the cuffs and raised them a few inches. "You forget the answers?"

The man grunted.

"Your boss's name." Jay straightened and closed in on the man.

He swore. "You'll get more of the same if you started bullying me."

Gates lowered the cuffs and raised them again.

Hammond laughed. "What? You think a few

exercises gonna break me down?"

"Not at all." Gates went through the process once more, lifting the hands a little highter. "But the break is much cleaner when the muscles and tendons have been stretched."

"You're gonna break my arm?"

"Don't worry. I know a pretty good doctor." Gates scoffed. "Course with one arm wrapped against your chest, you won't have much luck in defending yourself against the other inmates. Pity."

"Inmates?" Hammond struggled as Gates lowered and raised his hands once more. "You got nothing on me."

Jay's superior gave him look. His turn to persuade. "Thirty years minimum for an attempted murder of an officer. The premeditation will lengthen that. And the paint on your truck's grill, the paint from my car, nails you to the crime."

"Huh-uh. Someone borrowed that truck."

"With only your prints in the cab? *Only* your prints." Jay relished the horrified look that grew across the man's whiskered face. "What? Didn't you notice when your boss got in with gloves on?"

They'd broken him. His expression became transparent. Gates nodded lowering the cuffs a final time. "I want a name."

"He'll kill me."

"He'll kill you anyway. At least you have a chance if we have him in custody." His superior lowered the man's wrists. "Or do you really want to be a sitting duck in jail while the man who set you up has all the power and money to finish you off before you can implicate him?"

The man heaved a giant breath and, with the exhale, lowered his face to his chest. "Charles Bruton."

The lieutenant shouted for an officer to get a warrant for the man.

"You gotta protect me. He'll kill me. Like he tried to kill you."

Jay's face heated. "Why?" He grabbed the man's tee shirt in both fists, near his collar. "Why did you and your boss try to kill me?"

"The coat." Hammond's voice raised several tones. "The cleaning mark on the coat woulda pointed to Charles. Had his address connected to it."

Jay pushed off the man and took a step back. As they'd figured, but murder was extreme for so small a reason. "And Tonio?"

"Well, he had to die. First, he left his jacket to be found. That was stupid, man. But then he stole the take."

Something didn't make sense. "What?"

"What we got from Bella Nodo. Tonio musta hid it before Charles cut him. Anyway, we got a mile away and realized the bag wasn't in the van."

"Wait, why would Tonio put a target on his back like that? He'd have to know he'd put his life in danger."

The man squirmed and leaned against the brick behind him. "Charles thought it was something about a girl they both knew. Said he'd deal with her later."

Jay went cold. Dani knew this Charles fellow, too? Jay only got a glimpse of him when he was standing by his car, but he could have been one of the waiters. Had Tonio taken the stolen goods to distract Charles from bothering Dani? The possibility of a crook having any self-sacrifice in him seemed ridiculous, but the facts seemed to point that way. Maybe Dani had been more than an acquaintance? "I guess with Tonio's death, Charles collected his goods."

"No. Didn't have anything on 'im 'cept that book that belonged to the girl. Charles thought she must have the stash somewhere."

Jay turned to another officer. "Don't let that guy out of your sight." He darted for his partner's car. "Cal!"

The man came into view, jogging from the truck cab. "What's happened?" He puffed, but fell into step beside Jay.

"The boss thinks Dani has his money."

Cal hit the unlock on his key fob as Jay broke away from him toward the passenger side. For all of their hurry, they might already be too late.

Chapter Seventeen

Dani barely had time to punch in the speed-dial to Jay's number before Tasha called her back. "Is this you, Tasha?"

"He let me go." She sounded strange, not like herself at all. But with the panic and her heavy breathing, the words were broken and barely coming through.

"Get as far away from him as you can. Someplace busy and populated." With Tasha's height challenges, she could practically get lost on a school playground. "And put a wrap over your hair, a scarf or something." The blond corkscrews did have a tendency to stand out.

"No crowds... here." Her breath came in roars. "Warehouses."

"I'm coming to get you." Dani grabbed her sneakers and stopped to slip one on.

"I don't know... where...."

"What is a street name?" She shoved the other sneaker on her foot as she stood, teetering.

"I'll... call back."

Before the call ended, another rang in from an unknown number. This would be the guy wanting Dani's address. She set the phone on the coffee table and squatted to tie her shoes. The rings stopped after four, likely kicking into voice mail, but the phone started ringing again almost immediately. With Tasha wandering around lost, she couldn't risk the guy going after her again. She picked up the phone and hit the accept button. "Hello?"

"There. See? I'm a man of my word. I've released your friend, and I happen to know she's already contacted you."

He could only be guessing that. "Smart move. Now for you to turn yourself in."

"What you may not understand is that your friend is in my sight. Or should I say, sights."

Dani didn't miss the shooting terminology.

"So, Sammi dear, I suggest you don't delay any further. I want your address."

The repetition of her real name sent a streak of ice down her spine. Was this the man from whom Tonio had tried to protect her? "And you'll leave Tasha alone?"

"I would never have bothered your dear friend for an instant if you hadn't attached yourself to that cop. Most unbecoming. And you, practically married to someone else."

She gasped. She didn't recognize the voice, but this man knew her. Knew who she'd been.

"Your address. Now, please!"

Swallowing hard, she gave him the street and apartment number. She'd need to get as far away from home as possible.

"And you'll be there when I arrive."

"Of course." She'd had enough practice lying that the words held no quiver or hesitation.

"Good, because I've got some insurance with your friend."

Insurance? Did he have someone watching Tasha, ready to grab her again? "You promised that you would leave her alone."

"I will. As soon as our business is through."

"I have no business with you." Unless he'd been paid to stop her from making it to the trial in a few months.

"Ah, but thanks to our friend, Tonio, I have business with you." He paused for a moment. "Now, I assume you and I will be, shall we say, alone. Wouldn't want to bother the local authorities or that rather intimidating boyfriend of yours. I scare easily."

If he did have someone watching Tasha, she'd better act fast to get to her friend before this man found she'd left the apartment.

"And seriously, Sammi, do wait for me. You can't possibly make it to your friend before I reach your place. After all, I know where I'm going and you, sadly, do not. A few of my buddies are currently keeping an eye on the blonde. If I fail to contact them in a timely manner, they'll kill her. So if I find your place empty, or worse, full of cops, Tasha is as good as dead."

That blew her plans. "I'll be here." At least she could call Jay and alert him to the situation.

"With that, I bid you adieu, my dear. For the moment. But you must shut down your phone when you hang up. I'll be checking."

"My phone?" She put her call on speaker phone and went to the texting link. "Why do I need to shut down my phone?"

"I don't want any surprises. You will turn it off and leave it off."

After entering Jay's number, she typed in a short message. *Come quietly. Tonio's killer has*

Tasha in sights. "It's not like I'm going to put Tasha's life at risk." Although that's exactly what she would do if she sent Jay her message. But if she didn't, she'd be the dead one and justice would never be served. She rolled her lips in between her teeth.

"Don't forget that. I'm in charge and your friend's life is in my hands. Now end this call and turn off your phone."

She hit the send button. "Okay. I'll do that now." She waited a two-count before hanging up. By then, her message had officially sent. Or at least her cheap phone declared that it had. The phone rang immediately. He'd called back.

Answering, she didn't give him a chance to fuss. "I'm turning it off right now."

"Do it." The man roared through the line.

Dani started and dropped her phone on the carpeted floor. Snatching it up, she held the button to let it power down. What was she doing? Waiting here for someone to come kill her? This was insane.

Tucking her phone into her pocket, she darted for the front door.

Jay put in a call for back-up at Dani's apartment while Cal maneuvered through the remainders of the early rush hour.

"No one in a hurry this morning. Tires musta melted in the heat." He turned on his siren and switched on the blue strobes hidden inside his grill. "Maybe I can convince them to move."

Cars parted, but not fast enough to Jay's satisfaction. Dani didn't even realize she was in danger. He pulled out his phone, though he'd had little success in reaching her.

Still in his hand, the phone whistled, the tone he'd set for Dani's texts. He punched in his code and pulled up her message. "Uh-oh." Grabbing the dashboard mic, he adjusted the back-up request. "Have them go in quiet, park north of the complex, and meet me at the back on foot. Possible hostage situation."

And if he was reading this right, Dani was setting herself up. Again.

"Trouble?"

"Just got a text from her. Something about Tonio's killer having Tasha. But Dani wants us to go to the apartment." He reached for the light switch. "Hey, shut that noise off."

"You wanna get there quick or not?"

"She said come quietly." He let out an exasperated exhale. "I guess leave it on until you get closer, but not too close."

"How was she able to text you if there's someone there?"

"I don't know." Jay shook his head. He'd given up trying to figure her out. "But if she is with Tonio's killer—if she does have the take from the robbery like Hammonds said—there's nothing to stop him from killing her."

Dani flew to the door. At the very least, she'd run next door and put a call in to Jay. He had to know what to expect.

Flinging the door open, she nearly bowled into Tasha. "You're all right." She pulled her friend inside. "He didn't hurt you?"

"He? Who-he?"

Puzzle pieces swirled for a second before they came to rest in a different picture than she'd expect. "You lost your phone." This was bad. But there had been a woman calling....

Her friend's face brightened. "Did you find it? I thought I must have left it here, but I don't remember seeing it since before yesterday's job. I went to a movie, study break, so I didn't even think about it...."

The voice was so panicked and muffled from the heavy breathing, it could have been anyone. But it obviously wasn't Tasha. Dani took her roommate by the wrist. "We have to get out of here." She whirled toward the exit and yanked the door open to find the maître 'd from La Bella Nodo mounting the last stair.

"Going somewhere?" He lifted his blue hoodie to reveal a Beretta tucked into his waist band. "Unless you want to involve your neighbors, I suggest you... both... step back inside." He unzipped the jacket like he planned a friendly visit, but the eerie smile he wore and the piercing eyes spoke hate.

Dani stepped backward. "Take what you want. I have my purse over there." Dani eyed the man. A stranger except for the other night. Or maybe there was something about his black eyes. The crazy glimmer they held or the way he cocked up one eyebrow. Where had she seen that before?

"I will do that very thing." He spoke with exaggerated confidence and slipped off his jacket. Over his black pants, he wore a short-sleeved navy button down. A gold patch adorned one sleeve near the shoulder.

"Are you a cop?" Surely not, but his shirt looked like a uniform. Then her memory kicked in. "Wait. You were at Trudiano's this afternoon, working the scene."

"Funny how the officers, coming from so many different places, never question a stranger that seems to belong." He laughed. "With Tonio dead, I had to find another lead to where he stowed the cash. And there you were."

The cop had stood rather close when she realized Tonio was dead, but with his back to her. She'd only gotten a glimpse of his face as he left… right after Jay had decided to take her home.

"You stole Tasha's phone."

"Had to figure out where you lived—where you hid Tonio, but I couldn't follow you. Not with that indestructible cop driving you around. Both of you might have recognized me." He stepped closer. "Now, I've found you, *bellisima*." He ran the back of his fingers along Dani's cheek.

Her stomach threatened to empty.

He neared her face, concentrating on her lips. She stiffened and turned her head.

He halted an inch or less from her. His garlicky breath coated her skin like stale syrup. "Now, if you would be so kind as to hand over Tonio's bag."

What bag? She stepped to her right to put some space between them. "Tonio was hurt. I patched him up." Wait, there had been a duffel.

Without warning, he roared and shoved her against the wall. "That will get you killed." He pinned her with his forearm to her throat.

Dani kicked and coughed as the pressure increased. "I can't...." She tried to pull at the rock that made up his arm muscles and then struck out at his face, but missed. Her closely trimmed fingernails wouldn't have done any damage anyway. "Let...."

Tasha dashed to the kitchen and returned with a fire extinguisher hoisted over her head. "Let her go." She slammed it against the man's head.

He let go of Dani, screamed an expletive, and backhanded her roommate.

Dani went down on one knee, gasping for breath and fighting dizziness. *Get up.* Tasha was no match for this guy. Not alone.

By the time she looked up again, Tasha was a rag doll crumpled in a mass near the kitchen entrance. But Dani only got a glimpse before the man grabbed her by the hair and shoved her toward the closed door of Tasha's bedroom. "This where you're hiding my money?"

A tiny cry escaped. "I don't have it."

"Liar." He shoved her head first toward the door, but she put out her hands before she slammed into it. "Tonio didn't have it, so you have to." He rushed to her again and grabbed her chin with one hand, pulling his other fist back. "Where is it?"

I don't know poised on her tongue, but she bit it back. The truth would only buy her a busted nose or a chipped tooth. "In my room. He was in my room." She pointed to the open doorway on the perpendicular wall.

He dragged her toward it, digging his fingers into her cheeks. "Now that's the Sammi I know, even with the ugly hair." He shoved her onto the bed.

"I don't know you at all."

"Aww. That hurts, doll. That's really cold." His formality and the foreign hint of accent disappeared.

Doll? Only one man ever called her that. A shaggy-haired freak that even Robert hadn't trusted. "Bruton?"

"Ah. So you do remember." He slid his hand over his shiny head. "Like my new look?"

She remembered Charles Bruton all right. He'd knifed a partner over an argument about a girl that neither of them even knew. She almost went to the cops over that one, but she'd been persuaded to let others handle things, so she wouldn't be in danger.

Like now.

The smile slipped from Bruton's face. "I don't

like yours either. Now where's my money?"

"He was only in here. I wasn't with him the entire time." She got down on her knees and checked under the bed. He'd had a duffel. Army type, and she'd shoved it under her bed.

"Stop stalling, girl." He advanced on her.

She straightened and slapped her palms against her thighs. "If you want me to find it, give me a chance to look." Maybe her shouting would alert one of her neighbors.

"Shut up." His whisper felt even deadlier than his roar. "Check the closet."

She pulled the door open, causing her wool coat which hung on a hook inside, to fall off and land on the floor. She reached for it.

"Stop stalling." He picked it up and flung it across the room. "Green duffel."

The shelf above her clothes revealed nothing. She knelt and pushed aside her shoe tree. What were her winter boots doing next to her sandals? They belonged in the back... She reached for their traditional corner. The scratch of heavy-duty canvas met her fingertips. "I think I…"

With both hands, he shoved her aside and reached into the area where she'd been. Turning over the metal rack of organized shoes, he yanked out the bag along with a dress and a couple of slacks on their hangers. He tossed them to the floor. "Now we're talkin'."

Dani struggled to her feet. "Now, leave, like you promised."

He ignored her and fussed with the zipper.

A shadow passed near her window. She made sure Bruton was firmly engrossed and stole a glance outside. Jay's face appeared, his finger to his lips and his gun raised.

Thank you, Lord.

Bruton finally succeeded in unzipping the bag. "Ahh. This is it." Purses and wallets filled the open space. Then he cursed again as he dug deeper. "They're empty!" He threw the bag to the floor and turned a glare on her. "So you didn't even know it was there, huh?" The hatred in his face froze her to the carpet.

Grime Spree

Chapter Eighteen

Jay had sent two officers through the front door only seconds before he'd caught Dani's eye. Then Charles Bruton started roaring. Timing was off. The men wouldn't be in position yet.

But that's why he and Cal had stayed outside.

"Going in, kid." Cal had brought his flashlight with him to break through a window if necessary.

It was necessary.

The man inside flung a line of expletives at Dani before belting her with his full fist. At that moment, the other part of the team yelled while coming through the door.

Charles turned toward the window and grabbed a gun tucked into his waistband.

"Gun." Jay didn't need to say it any louder than a whisper.

Cal brought the heavy barrel through the glass and then ducked to the opposite side as a burst of shots fired from within the room.

Jay ducked into the opening on his knees and fired once, catching the man squarely in his forehead as two other shots rang out, probably from the officers behind him.

Bruton froze for an instance, hatred and determination painting his expression before his knees buckled and he landed on his back, his unseeing eyes staring at the ceiling.

"Stand down, Hunter." Cal raised his hand toward Jay.

His muscles, taut and neck stiff, he noticed he still pointed his weapon through the gaping hole.

"Clear." The officer inside, Ruidosa, lifted the muzzle of his gun along with his other hand.

"We've called in an ambulance, Sergeant."

Felt like he had to break through a layer of ice to finally make his joints release and his muscles lower his weapon. He holstered it and struggled to stand. "Dani."

Cal cleared off the jagged glass, and Jay followed him inside.

"One in here." Ruidosa led Cal to the other room.

Dani moaned as she lay against the wall. She bled from a thin cut under one eye and her cheek was swollen like she'd had her wisdom teeth extracted.

"Aw, honey." He put his hand on her shoulder as she tried to push up. "No, don't move." Leaning over her, he stroked her hair from her face and kissed her forehead.

"Tasha."

"There are people with her." He leaned back. "Cal?"

His partner poked his head through the door.

"She took a pretty hard hit, but she's beginning to come around."

Dani relaxed in his arms. "I knew you'd come, Sherlock."

He glanced at the bald head of the man he'd just shot. Lead settled in his stomach. He'd not had a choice. Bruton would have killed him or Cal. Dani might have become a target. Still, taking another life. He wrapped his arms around his girl and buried his face into her hair.

Dani's head screamed with every movement, but she kept her mask in place. The relaxed smile and her slightly raised eyebrows had finally convinced the doctors to let her leave the hospital. She could keep up the display at least until she crawled into the back seat of Cal's car.

Tasha seemed her normal self, though with a slightly purple cheek and eye, chatting with the handsome nurse who pushed her wheelchair. She practically beamed when the man suggested they meet for coffee over the weekend.

At least he wasn't a doctor. She wouldn't be in danger of having dates broken every time there was some sort of an emergency.

Jay's hand rested on her shoulder in the elevator and she covered it with one of her own. Broken dates or not, the man was a hero. *Her* hero. Her heart knew the truth every time he smiled at her, and nothing—not Matthew, not a crime syndicate, not threats on her life, or her secrets— would change that. At least not for her. Not even traveling to meet his family next weekend, though the thought of the encounter terrified her about as much as staring into crazy Charles's face.

The dimmer lighting of the covered drive, especially in the ebbing sunset, soothed her eyes. Much better than the stabbing illumination of the ER Trauma cubicle. Surely when she closed her eyes, the pain would become a dull ache. Jay helped her out of the wheelchair while Cal pulled his car into the covered drive. Tasha's giggle echoed against the high stone arch.

A heavyset man with the latest Ecos camera jogged forward. "This the lady who solved the restaurant robberies?" The loud call was accompanied by a flash and a squeal from Tasha.

The media? Really? Another flash. Thankfully, the guy seemed to be aiming more at her roommate than at Dani.

"No more pictures, please." Jay stepped in front of the photographer.

"How about an interview." Another guy advanced from a TV truck that pulled in behind Cal's car.

"They've had a long day already." Jay put his hand up for the guy with a news camera.

"We'll make them both stars of the ten o'clock newscast." A brunette woman with a microphone strolled forward with a sultry sway.

Jay paused. Dani looked from him to the

woman and back. She couldn't blame him for the hesitation. The reporter had perfect legs that she put on display with a flirty skirt begging for a Marilyn Monroe moment and a sleeveless blouse that showed more cleavage than material.

"Denise Staulmeyer, Channel eight. How did you happen to have possession of the stolen money, Miss Foster, and why weren't you arrested?" She shoved her microphone between her and Tasha as a bright light appeared and threaten to split Dani's skull.

"Now hold on." Jay pushed the camera lower and glared at the woman. "Don't go building your own fantasy Ms. Staulmeyer. You'll see the official report in the morning like everyone else."

Cal opened the back door and helped both of them inside before shutting it. "Nothing to see here."

Dani kept her face to Cal's back as he stood guarding her window. Another flash came from the other side, but the camera there had no view except of a mass of Tasha's blonde curls.

"Sorry about that." Jay got into the passenger seat. "You two all right?"

"Sure." Dani mustered another smile and belted her waist before resting her forehead on her palm.

"You don't look all right." Tasha peered at her friend.

"Shhh." She only needed rest.

Jay took another look at the disappointed Denise Staulmeyer. False accusations and petty insinuations to stir up responses marked a journalistic novice. She didn't appear to be a beginner, but her tactics revealed her as an amateur at best, and a vulgar one at that.

"Why would you even give that reporter another glance?" Cal started up the engine. "She's a freshly-painted ruin."

Dani hadn't heard his comment, had she? He pulled down the sunshade and used the mirror to check on her. With her head down and her bangs covering most of her face, she didn't react like Cal's comment had carried. "I wasn't exactly giving her my attention. More like disgust."

"Good, 'cause you got the right lady back there, buddy boy." His volume dropped and he thumbed the back seat just before he turned onto a busy road. He went on to share several details about past experiences with reporters like Denise Staulmeyer.

Jay already knew the truth of Cal's words about Dani, though. She had everything—brains, a devoted spirit, more natural beauty than Denise Staulmeyer - Channel 8, and a spunk that he'd never thought a girl with her looks could have. Every time he was around her, he found something else that he… well, that inspired him.

No that wasn't quite right. Maybe, encouraged him. What? Like his science teacher? That wasn't it at all.

He looked in the mirror again and took in the way her hair curled just enough to give it personality. She lifted her head slowly and pushed her bangs back so that they framed her face. Catching his eyes on her, she smiled and mouthed "I'm okay."

No doubts. The woman had his heart.

Tasha asked her a question and she turned to answer, but Jay kept her in view.

She enchanted him. Whether by the brilliant way she solved issues, or the courage that she showed in the face of death, she completely overwhelmed him in a way he'd never before experienced.

He loved her. It washed over him, filling his chest with yearning. A grin spread across his face.

She was indeed the right lady. He'd never been so sure of anything.

"Where'd that reporter get her name already?" Cal startled him out of his realization with the troubling question.

"Neighbors? I mean Staulmeyer or her little minions would have had several hours while we were in the hospital." Surely her name getting out wouldn't be a problem. It wasn't like anyone else, besides Charles, had a reason to be looking for Dani.

"Too many people got scanners. They hear too much. Stick their noses in." Cal wiped his nose as a sort of punctuation.

Tasha clicked her tongue. "The woman is a peacock. All pretty and alluring, then pecks at your eyes when she finally gets close enough."

"Still and all, we better keep a close eye on these two for a few days." Cal's voice reduced to a whisper while the women talked about news personalities in the back seat.

"Why?" Of course he would. Keeping an eye on Dani was his great pleasure, but why would Cal think they should.

"Just a thought." The man's neck pinked over

his wrinkled yellow button-down. "Better to be forewarned, you know."

Jay again watched her in the reflection. She stroked her still-swollen cheek. She turned toward the front and caught him staring. "How long was I at the ER?"

"A few hours." Jay closed the mirror and pushed the visor into place. "But you'll be glad to know that Tyrone and another team has already cleaned your place."

"Isn't it a crime scene?" Even without seeing her, he could picture the cute little curl that formed in her brow when she didn't understand something.

"Yeah, shouldn't it be?" Tasha chimed in from behind Cal. "A dead man and a bag of money. That would seem like a crime scene."

"Was. Not anymore." Cal didn't take his eyes from the road. "Only crime there was assault from the guy who was killed."

Happy he'd turned the reflection away before the change in topics, Jay rubbed one heated cheek with his cool fingers and moved the air vent to blow directly on his face. His mask was way too transparent, and he'd always been a lousy liar. She'd know at one glance how much killing that man affected Jay.

"The man was a psychopath bent on murder." Cal gave him a sidelong look. "Don't you dare regret."

Jay sighed. Of course he regretted any death. Especially a person who was lost, by all reasonable accounts.

Cal turned into the lot at the girls' apartment. "But I don't get what your friend, Tonio, did. After all that trying to protect you, why did he tell Charles where he hid the money?"

"He didn't." Dani replied. "Bruton saw me leave with him."

The memory of Tonio's bruised face came into view in Jay's mind. Thank goodness Dani hadn't had to see that. "He did protect you as best he could." And Jay would never let her know why he believed that.

Cal parked the car and gave a hand to Tasha while Jay helped out Dani.

She attempted a sad smile. "He protected me all right, but Tonio simply wasn't as good at it as you are."

With half of her face swollen, her smile would have been comical had he not realized how painful the action must have been. He wrapped one arm around her waist and held her close as they followed Cal and Tasha up the steps.

Her roommate paused on the landing. "The guy told us what happened, though. He pretended to be a cop to find out who Tonio knew."

"Makes sense." Cal moved aside as Dani advanced, digging the keys from her purse. "Somebody would have a connection, and the police would know it first, right?"

"Long shot, but I guess it was the only chance he had." Jay took the keys from Dani's shaky fingers.

"I guess he missed the discussion about my Bible." Dani accepted the keyring from Jay and led him through the doorway, flicking on the light switch.

"Yeah, he would have heard your name." Jay followed her in and made for the kitchen. "Mind if I help myself to some water."

"Go ahead." Tasha hung her purse on the doorknob that must've been her room. Obviously, not any worse the wear from her experience with Bruton. He pressed a glass against the water dispenser on the fridge. Dani, on the other hand, had her eyes half-lidded like it hurt to even have them open. He wanted to stay. Wanted to take care of her. Wanted to tell her all that he'd realized.

But exhaustion poured from those weary eyes.

He took a sip from the glass and set it in the sink. He and Cal needed to leave. Tasha could help her get some rest. "You both will need to make a statement tomorrow."

When he exited the kitchen, though, she'd had

a different thought in mind. She advanced on him, carrying the very same Bible that Madison had retrieved from Tonio's hotel room.

Chapter Nineteen

Dani flipped through the pages of her Bible. Tonio had been a crook, but he'd always been gruffly careful with her. "I think Tonio found his Savior. And I don't think he stole the money. I mean, he stole it at the restaurant, but I don't think he got away with it and left the empty bag here." She found the spot and turned the book for Jay to read the margin notes. "He left a note for me in my Bible."

"You have got to be kidding me." Tasha rushed forward with a chuckle. "Like some kind of treasure map?"

"Well, it's a good bet that his boss, Charles, wouldn't have found it." Jay looked down at the page. His face hard to read. The note was hardly intimate. But a shadow of something—anger, or maybe jealousy—crossed his features. "The bag's in your court now."

"The bag. He left it here. He told you about it." Tasha practically bounced.

"The bag was in the bottom of my closet. Between my boots and my running shoes."

"So what about the rest of it." He pointed to the note and put his arm around her.

Court? October? No. She couldn't explain. "Uh…"

"Why would he care about the weather getting colder?" Cal leaned over Jay's shoulder.

Colder? That was the point. Not October. She stepped back quickly. Pain screamed through her head and she put both hands to her temples.

Jay reached for her as she swooned. "You need to go back to the hospital."

"I'll be fine." She pushed off of him and made for her bedroom with Jay a step behind. "Colder." She opened the door of her closet. "My coat." The over-the-door hook that had held it was empty. That's right. Charles had thrown it in the corner.

She stumbled to the other side of her bed, but it wasn't there.

Jay caught her around the waist. "Honey, something's wrong. You should go back."

"Jay's right, Dani." Tasha stopped at the doorway with Cal holding up the facing on the other side. "You're not yourself."

She hadn't been for so long now. Or maybe she was. Maybe this new Dani was who the old Sammi had always been but never knew? She could live with that.

"I never leave my coat out in the summer."

"You never leave anything out. Any time." Tasha laughed. "Fair warning, Sergeant Hunter."

"Like I didn't already know her neat-nick ways." He shot her a tender look. "But I'm missing something. Why do you need your coat? It's July?"

"Exactly. My coat should not have been there, but it was." She pointed to the hook. "That hook holds whatever I'm using most often. In the summer, my swim suit and beach towel."

"She's right." Tasha moved to her closet and began sifting through the front rack to reach the one in back.

Jay side-stepped Tasha and replaced Dani's Bible on her night table.

Dani squatted and lifted the bed-skirt. Nothing. What had happened to her coat? "The only person who could have put my coat on the hook was Tonio. That's why he made the crack about cold weather."

"If it was in the corner, someone must've hung it up." Tasha reached into the back section of the packed rack. "Here." She pulled the black, full-length wool from the corner and handed it to Dani.

It was heavy. Enough to make the plastic hanger appear to almost break. This was a thick wool coat, but not that weighty. She poked her hand into the right pocket and wrapped around a few of the items there. Withdrawing it, she opened her fist. Two Rolex watches and a variety of sparkling earrings.

"He hid the restaurant loot right here?" Tasha dug into the other pocket extracting what looked to be a sapphire necklace, another watch, and a Mont Blanc pen.

"I knew he couldn't keep it." Not after the talk she'd had with him.

"If only he'd turned it over to the police." Jay shook his head. "All of this might have been avoided."

"Tonio would probably be facing some jail time, but he'd be alive." Cal stepped in. "But this isn't all he got. The manager was forced to open the safe. In fact, according to one of the waiters at the last place, Bruton ended up killing the owner because he had a time-lock on the safe that wouldn't open."

Even with the contents of the pockets laying on

the bed, her coat felt heavy. There had to be something more. She laid it across her comforter. The lining was bumpy.

"You've got to be kidding me." Jay pushed down on one of the bumps. "He sewed it into the lining?"

As much as Dani felt the urge to rip into the coat, she stopped and pulled her seam-ripper from her desk drawer and went to work. Inch-thick stacks of bills had been taped to the lining of the coat in neat rows. Thousands of dollars.

"I'm going to have to take this coat to the station." Cal picked it up by the hanger and headed for the door.

"Finders-keepers, big guy." Tasha followed him but Cal only laughed.

"Your friend really did try to do right by you." Jay sat on the edge of her bed and pulled her toward him.

She sank onto the comforter next to him. "I hope that he did place his faith and trust in the message of Romans." In Christ and the grace and forgiveness of the cross.

"I hope so, too, Dani. But you're not responsible for the man's choices."

"And you're not responsible for Bruton's death." She looked into his eyes. If only she could make him believe her words, yet the doubt in his expression ran deep. "He made his choices, Jay. You only reacted in protection that you had to give."

"I love the way you encourage." He lifted her hand and kissed her knuckles and helped her stand. He led her back into the main room urging her to get rest and let Tasha fuss over her.

Dani only half listened. He loved something about her. She let the word sink in while half of her brain attempted to drown it in a pool of what-ifs. Would she ever be able to release her fears and allow herself to be the woman she wanted to be?

His.

Days later, Dani let her hand hang out of the passenger window of Jay's new, navy blue, SUV. The wind from the high speed balled in her hand and pushed it up and down depending on the angle of her palm. "So you grew up in hickville?" Dani laughed. At least her swelling had gone down enough for her to be able to grin. And with the careful touch of Tasha's concealer, she'd covered most of the remaining bruises.

"Prince of hickville." Jay kept his eyes on the smooth, curving road. "Actually, Marseille isn't the backwoods place you think. It's rather large as far as East Texas towns go. Even has a couple of colleges."

She gazed at the tall pines that had crowded in on the highway. "Hard to think of a city being out here."

"Not a city. But it was big enough."

"Let me guess, football quarterback." Had to

be with his athleticism.

"Nope, I did run track, though. Sprinter."

That didn't explain his muscular physique.

"The truth is I was a little more of a nerd."

"Oh." She drew her brows together in mock horror. "Oh, dear. You mean chess club?"

"Ha. We weren't smart enough to have a chess club. I was a roper." He leaned back and delivered the title before putting his gaze back on the road.

Dani mentally ran through the sports she knew. None of them connected. "A roper?"

"Goat roper." A cute dimple grew as he suppressed his smile. "Common slang for the Future Farmers and Ranchers Club."

"You have got to be kidding."

"Sorry ma'am." He tapped his brow and gave her a nod. "Happens to be the sad truth."

Maybe roping goats built up his arms and shoulders. "And did you compete with roping goats?"

He laughed out loud. "No. That's just what the

other kids called the rodeo crowd."

"Rodeo? Like riding broncos and cows?"

"Bulls. And yeah, but I excelled in the calf-roping."

She cut her eyes to his face. "As opposed to goats?"

"Cute." He slowed on a right hand curve and turned left over a series of metal bars embedded in the dirt.

"This is Marsailles?" Didn't look like a town. Looked like a small lake pitted in a huge forest.

"Marsailles is another ten minutes down the road." He steered around a large rock in the road. "This is my parents' place. The house is through that grove of pines over there."

Dani clamped her jaw shut as her mind-battle raged with worry over whether his mom and dad would like her and frustration because it would likely not matter once Jay found out who and what she was.

He came to a stop and pushed the transmission

into gear. He reached for her hand and gave it a squeeze. "You don't have to worry."

She took a deep breath. "Of course I do. What if they don't like me? What if they think I'm too short, or not smart enough, or too snooty?"

"They're going to love you."

Growling, she gripped her hands into fists. "How can you be so sure of that?"

"'Cause I love you." He cupped her cheek in his palm and commanded her gaze to meet his own. "I love you, Dani."

He…? Really? Her mind turned to mush as he moved in for her kiss and her worries faded.

Excerpt from Grime *Family* (Book #4)

Matthew Donaldson's name on her phone ID meant trouble. No, more like impending doom.

Dani Foster put the phone to her ear, trying to assume a light tone. After all, her boyfriend, Jay, shared the front seat of his new Tahoe with her. "I didn't expect to hear from you, especially not this weekend." She pressed her volume button down, hoping Jay hadn't heard even a hint of the other man's voice.

"You have to come in." Matt's typical monotone was brusque, all-business.

"Yes, I'm enjoying the break. Nice to get away from work for a few days." Matt had given permission. Surely he remembered where she had gone.

"Never mind that. There's been a slight change." His tenor voice wiggled a bit.

This wasn't good, but with Jay maneuvering the driveway of his parents' property in East Texas, there wasn't a lot she could do about changes. And hardly anything she could utter out loud. "That's right, I'll be here until Tuesday, so I really can't visit with you until then."

Jay pulled to a stop and glanced at her. "Everything all right?"

She nodded. "Insurance salesman." She muffled her whisper with her hand over the phone's speaker. Lying had become way too easy, but it still pinged her with regret.

Matthew blew his exhale through the speaker. "Fine. Have it your own way. But you need to know that our mutual friend is no longer at his current residence."

Ice slipped all the way up her spine and spread across her shoulders. *God, please don't let this start again.* "Well, okay. Um… I guess I'll have to get back to you on that. Maybe as I'm coming back into town."

"Make sure you let me know before you get here. Better yet, you stay in… Mayberry… until you hear from me."

She couldn't stay here. Couldn't put Jay's family in danger. And what if they learned about…? "That's going to be tight."

"Not playing with you. Do as I say." Matthew hung up the phone.

She let the phone droop from her ear and stared at a nameplate on the black dashboard of Jay's new car. "Sure will… I'll call you as soon as I'm back in town…. Yes, sir. And thank you." She slipped her phone into her over-sized bag and glanced at Jay. "Sorry about that." Sorry on so many levels.

Look for GRIME FAMILY at Amazon.

About Marji

Marji Laine writes about hope and redemption. Her characters, tangled in desperate situations, rely on authentic faith in God to carry them through treachery, betrayal, and impossible circumstances.

A "graduated" homeschooling mom of four, she now teaches a high school Bible study and aspiring authors at various workshops and writing conferences. She spends most of her time formatting and designing books for Write Integrity Press. She also helps those through Roaring Lambs Ministry tell their stories.

Living with her sweet hubby of 33 years and her two rescue dogs, Marji loves her jobs – loves writing, formatting, and building covers. But given the choice, she'd rather be laughing, playing games, or doing projects with her family where one-liners are a norm. While she enjoys recharging on her own, she loves being a little goofy with her kids and their friends or acting and singing from time to time on stage.

Content is probably the best description of me. I teach my kids to "enjoy where they are while they're there." A lesson in joy that I had to learn the hard way.

She prefers mountains to beaches, dogs to cats, entrees to desserts, and Jaguars to any other vehicle. Her favorites include emerald green, autumn, stargazer lilies and white roses, New York style pizza, and red velvet cake with cream cheese icing.

You can keep up with Marji by joining her monthly newsletter list at her website, www.MarjiLaine.com. And you can also find her at the WriteIntegrity.com website as well as on her Facebook Page.

From the Author

Dear Reader,

I'm beginning to feel like Dani and Jay are real folks. Like I might happen upon them at the grocery store or one of the nearby restaurants! I'm so enjoying telling their story.

While this episode revealed a little of Dani's history, her next will reveal all and bring her to a crisis of her faith.

Have you ever had one of those? A time when everything you believed, deeply held convictions, were tested by the circumstances you experienced? I've been there. It's so easy to sink into despair and allow confidence to evaporate.

This is the very reason why we have to stay close to the Father at all times, not only when tragedy or trials attack. Staying close to Him deepens the faith that will carry when those faith crises occur.

I'm praying for you, dear reader, that your relationship with your Father deepens each day and that your love for Him grows and expands throughout your life.

Special thanks to a couple of amazing writers who continue to inspire me to get on my computer and write like the wind. Jackie Castle and Patricia PacJac Carroll offer such encouragement and have been incredibly instrumental in my venture into independent publishing. I'm also thankful to some special readers: Christa Upton, who is an outstanding proof-reader, and Precious Redhead who questioned my story in just the right areas to make Grime Spree even better. I also appreciate the way my twins and dear hubby never let me give up on the desires of my heart.

And I thank my Father for allowing me to indulge in this passion to write and for His blessing on the stories.

Until next time, dear reader!

Be Blessed!

Marji

PS. Come visit with me at
MarjiLaine.com!

Other Books from Marji Laine

Grime Fighter Mysteries
A Complete Series!

Working as a crime scene cleaner is perfect for neat-nick Dani Foster who has recently been relocated by her witness security contact. But she can't hide the investigative reactions drilled into her by her detective father. Even though her discoveries, and the explorations they instigate, often put her into funny, uncomfortable, and sometimes dangerous positions.

Marji Laine

Heath's Point Suspense

COUNTER POINT – Book 1

Her dad's gone. Her business is in trouble, and her car's in the lake. Cat McPHerson doesn't have anything else to lose... except her life. And a madman is determined to take that.

Her former boyfriend, Ray Alexander, returns as a hero from his foreign mission, bringing back death-threats. Cat must find a way to trust Ray, the man who broke her heart or neither of them will survive.

BREAKING POINT – Book 2

Why would anyone want her dead?

Alynne Stone wanted nothing to do with her parents' inn after they left their lifelong home in Dallas to move to Heath's Point, Texas. Then an emergency phone call not only drew her to her parents' bed and breakfast, it thrust her into the crosshairs of a killer.

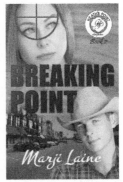

Lieutenant Jason Danvers has no idea why his kind and generous friend was killed. But the man's beautiful, prodigal daughter needs all the help he can give her to stay alive.

AIN'T MISBEHAVING

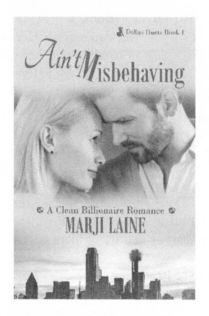

Book 1 of the
Dallas Duets Clean Billionaire Romance Series

Annalee Chambers: Poised, wealthy, socially elite. Convict.

She floated through life in a pampered, crystal bubble until she smashed it with a single word. Dealing with the repercussions of that word might break her, ruin her family, and land her in jail. That is, unless a handsome worker from the "other" side of the tracks, who has secrets of his own, can help her find her way.

Made in United States
North Haven, CT
26 October 2022